MW01181361

The Last Classroom

Dinah Havens

abbott press®
A DIVISION OF WRITER'S DIGEST

The Last Classroom

Abbott Press books may be ordered through booksellers or by contacting:

Abbott Press
1663 Liberty Drive
Bloomington, IN 47403
www.abbottpress.com
Phone: 1-866-697-5310

ISBN: 978-1-4582-0275-8 (sc)
ISBN: 978-1-4582-0276-5 (e)

Library of Congress Control Number: 2012904402

Printed in the United States of America

Abbott Press rev. date:3/6/2012

CHAPTER ONE

The sun was dissolving like a lozenge in a feverish child's mouth. It was a chilly spring evening. The air was freshly misty in Beachtown and a full moon started to appear over the small population with a string of moving clouds. You could hear dogs starting to bark as if they were communicating with each other.

There were a few suburban blocks named after kinds of horses. Thoroughbred, Clydesdale, and Arabian were some of them. They flanked a small main drag where there was the town square. Some statues made of concrete adorned it in a military setting. It showed George Washington holding a rifle aiming at a huge copper turkey. An iron fence with a gate similar to that of a cemetery surrounded the scene. The gate would slam shut at ten o'clock every night although clever pranksters would shoot their paintball guns at the statues, usually with orange paintballs.

A courthouse loomed nearby in a dark gray cloud of despair. Citizens would rather be at Bensen's Bingo Hall and Bar having some unforgettable times. Explosions of laughter could be heard from down the street of that cheerful place. The smell of sweet barbeque floated from on the other side of the square. It came from a quaint little café called Minnie's.

The sidewalks were of cobblestones that were in surprisingly good condition. The old, rickety post office remained just outside of the square in its Victorian style spookiness. It had once been new, but then got used as rental apartments, and then finally became the Beachtown Post Office.

This night was just exactly like most nights here- uneventful. Beachtown stayed forgotten most of the time with the exception of people coming off of Highway 5 to top and go to the dusty gas station. They would just gas up and leave. Sometimes the Beachtown Sheriff's deputy would sit in anticipation of a speeder or two. Usually, not a lot of tickets were issued. It was pretty slow paced at the police department, but ironically, there was no donut shop.

Even the farmers were scarce outside Beachtown. There was only one orchard on the only farm road. It consisted of apples and peaches. It was the town's source of fruit and was owned by a hardworking family. The children were still young. They enjoyed picking apples that were basketable. They also owned a small horse ranch called Brown's. Horseback riding lessons were offered by paid instructors who taught kids in a ring. Training for horse shows was a common goal for the teachers to have their students achieve. Some would make it to Nationals, and some even became champions of their class. Western and English were the main categories that could be practiced. There were about five horses that would be ridden and cared for by students at Brown's. Some students came from other small surrounding towns just to have lessons with the horses. Kids would arrive home smelling of fresh air and manure from the day's practice and cool down.

There was one school in Beachtown. It accommodated

grade school, middle school, and high school students all in one. The principal was the only one at the school for thirty years. Students received an education while getting a lot of attention in their small classes. Usually, if a student graduated from the whole school, they would have to move away from their families in order to go to a college in another town or city. There were no colleges in Beachtown, and a lot of graduates would become teachers or tutors if they had to stay. Any other job was hard to come across. One could start a small business, but many opportunities were non-existent.

The Mississippi River flowed muddily about five breezy miles east of town. You could hear coyotes howling at the full moon. From the beach, trout could be found flipping in a silverfish flourish. The air smelled of a salty sweet smell. An occasional beer bottle floated up to the shore. They were probably thrown carelessly by a teenager. A bum may have done the same thing. Crawfish liked to crawl up on rocks to greet a fisherman or woman. Tonight, the river sighed without a person to hear it. It flowed freely without criticism. It was a calm week night. The townspeople were busy winding down after a hard day. Nobody remembered the river at this time. They did not see the toads hop into the budding brush, or the group of deer coming out of the sycamore forest to get a drink. There was not anyone to hear the slurping does, or the owls whimper their nightly regrets. If somebody was there, they would notice some fog drifting above the water with bats darting across it, screeching all the way. Someone missed a bear come out of hibernation to look for a fish to claw out of the water. It growled at a group of robins flying away because they were startled. Their branch slapped against the leaves of another as they split. The river was so wide and vast that the other side looked foggy and dark. Some fallen trees protruded in blackness on the shoreline but they were barely visible. Many catfish had been caught there by families out on a picnic. Fisherman baiting their lines had many good days. This enormous body of water was alive with its very own ecosystem. It had a very unique way of balancing itself. If there were too many guppies, then fish would eat those baby toads. Water moccasins would take care of any overpopulated trout community. Too much algae would be devoured by mosquitoes and little silvers. Worms might be enjoyed by catfish.

It had not rained in the past week so the river was in no way overflowing. It was just righteously flowing along at a pleasant, peaceful pace. It moved freely like blood in the veins of one who had good blood pressure. There were no clogs that could be seen looking upstream or downstream. It was too early in the year for crickets to be chirping yet. A couple of hawks called to eachother, maybe spotting a rotten animal along the side of the river. Buzzards must not have come this way tonight. Box turtles and terrapins had to take care not to get their heads and feet bit off because they liked the wet sand on the beach and did not want to hide all of the time.

Some pine trees blew in a strong breeze as pinecones fell to the earth softly. They were the remaining ones to come off after winter. Nearby, an earthworm pushed itself across the dirty floor of mud. It wiggled around in its fleshy wetness until a female cardinal swooped down on it. Its beak picked it up and the bird smacked it with satisfaction. That worm should have stayed underground with the other various kinds of worms and slugs. Sometimes they did make their way over the ground. Slugs liked to slime themselves to a rock for a new kind of journey. Maybe they would search for insects to eat, dead or alive. As gross and disgusting as they were, still, at least they could be brave.

This did not exclude mutated species. There were a small amount of toads and frogs that had three back legs. Some had three front legs. Even a smaller amount of frogs had three back legs and three front legs. They were the champion swimmers of the whole river. With more leg muscles, they could paddle faster, especially if they got frightened.

Frogs were not the only species to have abnormalities. Mutation was not limited to frogs or toads. Fish sometimes were born with an extra tail or fin or both. Some fishers were pleasantly surprised when they caught a fish like that. They would want to take them home to mount on their wall. When their friends would come over for dinner or something, they would see this and be amused. Tonight, though, there would be no surprises like that. All the fish here would remain alive. Nobody would be making a spectacle of anything. All was silent except for the toads croaking their nightly news to eachother. A rabbit hopped near the beach out of some milk thistle. It stayed still until a mean old blue jay screamed at it. The rabbit dashed off, startled by the bird's rude tone. Little did they know, a snake had made its way into the scene. It was about four feet long, and about four inches wide. It slithered near where the rabbit left, smelling it still. Red and black spots with gold around them shouted a warning to any being that saw it. It was a hungry snake trying to find food. The blue jay, not noticing the snake in the dark, flew to the ground. Before the bird knew, it was being enjoyed by the snake's quick mouth. Being just an appetizer, it now had to go through the snake's long body. Although it ran away, the rabbit was lucky because snakes would prefer one over a blue jay bird for a meal any day. The reptile slowly went into the woods close by, whether it was content or not. It needed to find either a warmer place to go digest, or to find some more to eat. Its tongue made a sipping sound going in and out of its mouth.

The wind picked up as the night went on towards midnight. The full moon was still visible but it was higher in the sky and smaller. It was looking like a brightly glowing pearl up there in its beautiful orbit. The clouds had mysteriously cleared away, leaving it naked.

A spider fell to a sycamore leaf below its tree. It had descended down from its tiny cotton candy-like string. It had spent all night working on a nice-sized web. Hexagonal and sticky, it was waiting for an insect or insects to fly into it. This brown spider was hungry just like all of its neighboring creatures. A ladybug soon enough unknowingly flew its spotted self into the spider's trap. Before it knew anything, it had to come to realize that it was stuck. It squirmed and kicked but could not fly free of the trap. It was glued there, suspended in the air. Remaining there, it was going to have to wait until it was eaten by the spider. Other unsuspecting insects were surely going to come to the same natural and unlucky situation.

All of a sudden, a walking stick jumped from out of nowhere only to land in the spider's dinner quarters. It was just a young, small one, so it did not weigh enough to fall through onto the ground. It looked to be caught right next to the poor ladybug just as or if not more puzzled than she! Unfortunately, it would not blend in with that background. In silent terror, the insect tried to jump out of that horrible trampoline. It almost succeeded, only to fall down still hanging from the tangle of death. Thrusting around, the walking stick finally fell down to the dirt. It quickly evacuated itself back into the gray trees.

Further into the forest of leafless trees, a possum had its pink tail wrapped around one of the lower branches of one tree. It was hanging from it in a deep sleep. It looked like a cross between a big mole and a huge rat. As it dreamed, its bland ugliness fit in with the brown-gray botanicals of early spring sycamores. A snail dragged its small shell up the possum's tree with its antennae ready to sense anything.

There was a clearing even further into this arborized world, with a small pond in the center. It was the color of light green. Lillypads resting on top of the surface blended right into the pond. Little frogs looked like they were jumping across the water but were actually using the lillypads as stepping stones. An ellipse of little flies was hovering above the middle of the water. A toad came up to the air and whipped its tongue out to catch however many flies would stick to it. Its tongue rolled back into its mouth quickly, and the toad seemed satisfied for the brief moment. Then , the amphibian dove back into the algae and on under the water.

A few fish existed here, too. When a toad would have tadpoles, the fish would get excited once they found this food. There was an ambivalence about the pond. One day, it said a baby toad could live and be content, and the next day the pond would change its mind and have the tadpole turn into a snack. Nothing seemed to stay the same for any creature here. Every day held many surprises, yet made no promises.

As the night approached the wee hours of the morning, some stars were shining brighter. A meteor shower took place above the woods, some chunks of space rock falling into the atmosphere, burning up before they could reach the tops of the trees. It made a pretty show. The people of Beachtown close by might have seen it if they were awake.

The earth was starting to greet the sun as the sky slowly turned a milky blue. A group of blackbirds crowded over to the pond squawking on the way. Not finding what they were looking for, the team flew away together, making a pattering sound with their wings. A couple of squirrels ran past, then stopped and flicked their fluffy tails. Up a tree they went, not stopping until they were out of view, up high. A patch of small white flowers made itself comfortable under the tall tree. Spring was starting to make itself known. Some newborn baby robins were waiting in their nest in a neighboring tree. Their beaks were open wide in anticipation of their mother bringing them some worms. The remainder of their sky blue eggshells lay on the earth below the budding sycamore.

Toward the river, a bear the size of two refrigerators growled an unpleasant growl. It was looking out on the river where a couple of rafters were floating lazily down the river with a pack of beer. They were laughing at the bear who kept on growling in disapproval. The bear glared at them until they passed on down the river.

"That was spooky.", said one of the rafters.

"Yeah, that bear was mad, dude.", the other rafter responded drunkly.

"Okay, let's get out of this river before we get to that factory a few miles down the way. It stinks way too much. Like big time waste.", said the first rafter.

"Okay, I'll go for that!", said the second rafter. They wasted no time in getting their raft out of the river. The bear kept on glaring at them, not forgiving them for laughing at him. A fish jumped high out of the water at that moment, and it flipped right into the path of the great bear and the bear showed teeth. It opened its big, stinky mouth and grabbed the fish with its huge canines and snarled all through its given feast. It seemed to be showing off to the rafters with blood and guts being spilled all down its furry chest that could just as easily be one of them. The rafters ran soberly with all their strength away from the river.

*   *   *

The factory protruded, with pollution coming out of its smoke stack, right near the huge, mysterious stream called the Mississippi. It was just a mile from its nearby town, Beachtown, Missouri. It produced burning smells, and could be smelled slightly from the post office of Beachtown.

The runoff was another fact of life for that factory. Property values were somewhat of a joke near this supposed facility. That was because it smelled like harsh sewage. One could even be indoors and not get away with not breathing in the stench. They would have to have a steady supply of air freshener. The air was not a fresh, sweet, and salty scent in this area. There were quite a few abandoned houses and buildings for understandable reasons. Nobody would want to be around this disappointing environment.

The smoke came into the Missouri air day and night; dawn and dusk. Only the poor lived near there, because landlords were lucky to find tenants to live in that spot. That is because the renters could practically taste the enormous eyesore. The only upside to this landscape is that the sunsets were immensely breathtaking. This is because the air was so polluted. Otherwise, the horizon was uglified by the smoke stacks from that stern gray establishment. Any being with a sense of smell would understandably avoid that part of the river.. It seemed that the river was a non-entity in the factory's setting. Putridity was an every day occurrence on these outskirts. The smell was sort of a rotten aroma. This factory farm and slaughterhouse had made an industrialized environment out of practically the middle of no place. It was the gates of doom for the river to enter as it flowed unknowingly along. When it rained, it downpoured polluted water on the life of the vicinity. This would explain the lack of farms outside Beachtown. Farmers wanted to yield healthy crops in other areas, without poison rain to soak them.

The sun was now up, and the people of Beachtown were reporting to work once again. The employees at Minnie's, for example, were parking their cars, to get into the kitchen to make up the fresh barbeque for the day. The same thing was taking place at the factory farm and slaughterhouse, except the workers were not quite happy about clocking in. Dread was in the air as the brave souls took on another productive day in the unit that scrimped on scenery.

CHAPTER TWO

Somewhere between the obtrusion and Beachtown was a small neighborhood with a dusty lane of gravel. Grasshoppers purred in the late morning sunshine as if they were happy. Occasionally they would spring to the side of the road when an automobile would drive through.

Sundial Road sort of wound its way around for a couple of blocks and then made a dead end in an imperfect cul-de-sac. The smell of fresh grass was a little thwarted by whiffs of a sewage smell. The houses on this road were built in the nineteen-thirties and were a little small. Many of them needed new paint. They all kind of looked alike with garages put more toward the back yards. The most bedrooms these cottage styled houses had were two. People living in them could not afford to move into anything more expensive. They felt that they were lucky to be able to finance the maintenance of their dwellings. Sometimes they had to make the most urgent repairs only and neglect the other improvements that could be made. This little neighborhood was largely forgotten by Beachtown. There would never come a day where asphalt was laid instead of gravel on Sundial Road. A stray dog that looked to be pure St. Bernard piddled amongst the houses, marking some random cars with itself. An old lady burst open her front door a few doors down and called "Tiny! Here Tiny!" Her buddy dashed to her voice, jumping over a small hedge, and went to his owner, whimpering and licking her as if he had not seen her for months.

"Good Tiny-boy. Good boy." the aged, loving woman reassured. She was about the warmest neighbor one could have on this lonely block. She gripped an oxygen tank with wheels. A spell of emphysema made it hard for her to breathe. She had never smoked a cigarette a minute of her life.

"Let's get inside, buddy. Want some doggie snacks?" the dog panted as if in agreement.

The front door shut slowly as the lady rolled her machine behind her.

Next door, in a two bedroom, one bath cottage, a mother and son sat in their cozy living room. The smell of chocolate overwhelmed the small house.

"I wonder how Ginny is doing next door?" asked the teenage boy with dark,curly hair. He was getting ready to graduate from Beachtown High with honorable grades.

"Good, I hope, sweetie." returned his mother, May, who was concentrating on hanging up a new picture on their wall. "You know, I need a hammer." she declared, pushing back her shoulder length blonde hair, and dashed to her well-organized utility room. She could get an award for her outstanding housekeeping knack.

The yard was also nicely done. For starters, the small tiled porch had some potted petunias freshly planted on either side of the arch-topped alder front door. Each window on either side of the porch had a flower box already cleared out for germinating. There were daffodils along the sidewalk coming up to the porch. Some ivy had grown on the house but May kept it under control. If she did not, it would grow wild and slowly tear up the wood siding of the creamy yellow colored house. Bermuda grass dominated the front and back lawn, becoming thicker and greener. There was one crab tree in the middle of the front yard, just about to blossom a pleasant light pink. Every year, yellow tulips would bloom in a circle around its tree trunk. There was certainly nothing brash about the landscaping.

The gravel driveway led to the one car garage. Inside was a Saturn two door with a standard transmission. It was a 1996 forest green with a decent tan leather interior. It was no limited edition, but it got Tooley and his mother from point C to point D. Usually, it was Tooley's mother that drove it to her job at the Beachtown Medical Clinic. She educated people about illnesses in meetings on certain days, and on other days she did clerical work in her office. She had been studying to become a nurse, but after her divorce she took some time off and continued working.

"Can I go to Ginny's and give her these chocolate chip cookies that I just finished making?" asked the respectful son, itching his facial scar put there by chicken pox when he was little.

"Sure, but I will be leaving for work in about half an hour." said his mother. Usually, she worked from about nine to four at the medical clinic.

"See you later, mom! I'll have our dinner planned when you get home." Tooley wanted to help his mother with the meals. He loved to cook anyhow.

"That's so nice of you, honey. I love you!" his mother paused at the front doorway with her stylish leather purse over her shoulder. Then she opened the door and walked off the porch and down the driveway to the garage. She did not have to lift the big garage door because she had a remote that opened the door when a button was pushed. The car was waiting for her. May got in and started it up like she always did every day. Backing out, she still had her finger on the button and stopped. The button was pushed, and the garage door shut automatically. She pulled the car down her driveway, and drove off down Sundial Road toward her place of employment in Beachtown.

Tooley, not wasting any time, took the fresh chocolate chip cookies in one hand and walked through the front door. He did not really have to lock the door . In this area, people were not so worried about leaving their doors unlocked.

He felt like whistling as he made his way across his yard into Ginny's. She had a bird bath to clean out and leaves to rake. It was turning out to be a really nice, warmer day. Tooley wondered if she needed some help with her yard this year. He got to the front porch and knocked on her plain, six panel front door painted red. While he waited, he could hear Tiny barking at the door as his master slowly got up off her dog-hairy couch. She, being an elderly person, moved slow so people had to be patient with her. Ginny finally opened the door. When she saw it was Tooley, her face lit up and she unlocked her screen door. "Come in, Tooley!" she exclaimed.

He entered her house, carefully standing next to her oxygen machine. "How are you doing, Ginny?" he asked.

"Oh, fine dear. What do you have here?" Ginny curiously asked with a pleased smile.

"I brought over some cookies just for you!" Tooley answered.

"Oh! What kind are they?" Ginny would have liked any type of cookie. She was having a good day.

"Your favorite-chocolate chip." Tooley hoped she would be happy with his cookies.

"Thank you! How nice of you to do that! I love chocolate chip cookies!" she declared, and gave Tooley a hug.

"Your welcome. It was no trouble at all. You are my favorite neighbor, you know." Tooley was glad that she appreciated the sweets.

"Come in and sit down, child! Do you want something to drink? A Coke?" offered Tooley's senior friend.

"No thanks, Ginny. I just came over to see how you were doing." Tooley came into the living room and sat down on the couch. He started to feel sneezy because he was allergic to dogs and cats.

"Well, I am doing okay today. My doctor told me I am too thin and need to eat more. He gave me a new medication for it so I can have my appetite back." she said and slowly sat down next to her young friend. "You graduating high school yet?" she wondered out loud.

"Yes, I graduate in May. I got all As on my last report card. I think I've beat Warren." he responded. "That is so excellent! You'll have to come over and celebrate. I know I don't have a lot but we could watch a movie this summer here. We could find something in my VCR library. You can pick any one out you want to see." offered Ginny.

"That sounds nice." Tooley said. He went on. "Ginny, are you going to need some help with your yardwork?"

"You know son, I just might. I am getting pretty languid." Ginny answered pleasantly.

"What's languid mean?" Tooley wanted to know.

"Oh, that means that I lack energy. I am probably not going to be very able at this point, but I keep trying." she explained with a sigh.

"Well, I will be around to help you if you need it. I can mow, rake, and even plant your flowers, but just let me know. I noticed the leaves out front. I could start raking." Tooley suggested.

"If you think you would like to, go right ahead. I will pay you what I can." Ginny agreed.

"Don't mention it." he was not interested in money necessarily.

Tooley looked around. Ginny had a basket next to her couch. It was filled with different colors of yarn: blue, black, green. and yellow. It looked like she knitted the big green and black blanket that was draped over the rather plain-looking divan. A half full glass of iced tea sat on the coffee table with a slice of lemon stuck on the rim, unsqueezed. The bulky television was not on. Her remote laid on the couch, almost ready to fall through the cushions. There was a cuckoo clock on the wall, about ready in ten minutes to start announcing the new hour. Tiny was laying on the floor next to Tooley's foot, comfortably snoozing and snoring.

"Ah-choo!" Tooley was getting allergic to Tiny's brown and white fur.

"Oh, dear, let me get you a tissue." Ginny slipped one out of its box from the end table next to where they were sitting. "There now." said the lady, handing it to the red-nosed boy.

"Thank you." Tooley was sniffing and took the tissue to wipe his irritated face." I guess I'll be leaving now, but give Tiny a hug for me." Tooley requested.

"Okay, sweetheart. You go now." Ginny was sympathetic.

Tooley got up and wadded up the tissue in his hand. "Okay, Ginny.

I'll see you soon. Have a nice day!" Tooley was out her door and into the spring day's fresh air. He thought that it was a big relief to get out of the stuffy, slightly dog-smelling little house. He walked back over to his front yard again and opened the front door. Tooley appreciated his house because it smelled fresher.

CHAPTER THREE

"I am dreading studying for that earth science test." Tooley thought to himself. He was not very confident that he was going to keep his A in that class. His teacher was nice but had a boring way of teaching. He wondered where his old notes were so he could get to work. A huge sigh came out of his mouth and went to the small kitchen to grab a Coke out of the General Electric refrigerator. Him and his mother had it for as long as he could remember.

Slurping his beverage, he walked back down the little hallway to his tidy bedroom.

"Okay." he said out loud, intending to get serious. He got in his black Nike book bag. It was stuffed with not only the earth science book, but with a few other books and notebooks. He had a few final exams to study for. Shuffling through a red notebook, he found all the notes that he needed to study with. Tooley sat at his small desk made of oak. May and he bought it at a yard sale last fall. Until that magic moment, Tooley had studied at the kitchen table.

"What is a metamorphic rock?" Tooley asked himself. He thought and thought. "Oh yeah, I know that without looking at my notes. It is a rock that changes through time." Tooley answered correctly, and he gave examples of those kinds of rocks. He already felt more confident. Tooley was a lot smarter thatn he gave himself credit for. His mother, May, noticed that about her son. Sometimes she would help her young man study. With her help, for example, he aced his algebra class in his freshman year. Tooley loved May for that and would never forget her careful tutoring.

The house was so silent that Tooley could hear the kitchen clock ticking all the way from his bedroom. About thirty minutes went by and he was nearly finished going through his earth science notes. The black phone in the kitchen started to ring. The straight A student got up from his studies and skipped to the kitchen wall next to the refrigerator. He picked up the receiver after the second ring.

"Yello?" Tooley said in a jolly voice.

"Tooley!" said a young voice.

"Hi, Warren." Tooley was not surprised to hear from his best friend."I just got done studying for my earth science final for next week. It's my first one." Tooley answered.

"I only have one final until graduation. It's my English IV final. It's going to be over that book we are finishing. I'm pretty nervous, but my GPA should still be what it was last semester." Warren stated. He was also an honor student and could even have graduated early. He decided to take his time. Besides, he wanted to graduate with his friends.

"What are you doing this weekend, Tooley?" Warren questioned.

"Oh, I don't know. Nothing I guess. You order your cap and gown yet?" Tooley was just making conversation.

"Yes, I did yesterday. I'll look like such a dork. All I want is the red and black tassle to hang up somewhere. I can't wait!" Warren exclaimed.

"Yeah, those gowns and caps seem pretty stupid, but I'll like hanging mine up in Mom's car." Tooley replied.

"Totally." Warren agreed. "You wanna go to my little sister's horse show in Sedalia? My parents will get us a motel room at Lodge Seven and we can party this weekend!"

"That sounds cool, Warren. Maybe I can if my Mom says it's okay." Tooley was excited. He did not really get into horse shows, but he wanted to maybe hang out with Warren. They had not had a class together throughout high school. "I'll call you in a couple of days and let you know what I'm doing." Tooley negotiated.

"Okay. Later." Warren hung up.

"Bye." Tooley hung up also. Yawning, he went back to his bedroom thinking about studying for his other finals. He decided not to because finals were not for a few more weeks. He stood there wondering what to do next when he remembered that he was supposed to plan dinner.

On the way to the kitchen, he went outside to the garage. He spotted a rake leaning up against the dirty wall. A trowel for planting flowers lay on the top shelf of May's bronze baker's rack. The lawn mower had been taken out of where it was against the other wall and put in the middle of the garage floor. May must have been getting it running for the new season. It appeared that Tooley had everything he needed to maintain their lawn as well as Ginny's. He was eager to start helping out. That meant that he could use the car on weekends or something. Then he wondered about this coming weekend. "Maybe if I studied enough, Mom would let me go." thought Tooley.

Tooley loved his mother very much. If he forgot something for school, his mother would drive into Beachtown to make sure that he had everything he needed, even if it made her late for work. When he broke his arm in the third grade, she let him stay home from school for as many days as he needed and would bring him his make-up work. If he misplaced his winter coat, she would make sure that he had one to keep him warm even though they were not rich. She always managed to keep the bills paid somehow, and Tooley was very appreciative for his age.

Approaching the kitchen pantry, Tooley thought of what to have with the meatloaf. He decided on green beans and a salad. He got all of his ingredients out and set to work on supper. Tooley even had the recipe for meatloaf memorized. It was something that he always enjoyed watching his mother make. He liked mixing everything up with his hands but did not know why. It just was fun.

As soon as Tooley was done, he put everything but the green beans in the old refrigerator. Later he would cook the meatloaf. It was not yet time for May to come home. Tooley thought that she would enjoy having dinner already made after a hard day at work. He thought of how viable she was and knew that making dinner was the least that he could do for her. It was when he was about ten that May gave him that extra key to the house for when he came home after school. As long as he could remember he was unlocking the front door at around 3:30 every day. Tooley learned responsibility at an early age. Since his parents split up at that time, he had to take care of extra things besides just school. Laundry and dishes were his main chores starting at fifth grade. May was having a really hard time and had to quit her studies to become a nurse. She was hoping that one day she could do a correspondence course and get her degree. Work became more necessary after the divorce to Tooley's father.

Tooley went back to his simple bedroom to turn on his gray and black boombox that played cds. He had bought it last summer doing several odd jobs around Sundial Road while waiting to collect enough coinage to upgrade to an iPod. He had just enough to get a new cd to listen to. He picked out one by a group called Korn. It was his only one. Tooley did not have a cd case or shelf. He just kept the lone cd on his nightstand. Today, he felt like listening to the schizophrenic lyrics. He loved them and wanted to get lost in some music in order to relax.

After listening to the entire cd, while laying down on his twin bed covered with his grandmother's hand sewn quilt, he wondered about Warren's invitation. He wanted to go, but hoped that he would not have to sit through Warren's little sister's English Pleasure classes. Warren and he probably would want to stay at the motel and swim, maybe they would sneak a beer from Warren's parents' cooler. Lots of people brought coolers with drinks and snacks in them to horse shows. It gave people a chance to socialize and to keep in touch with fellow horseback riders and their parents.

"Maybe Mom will let me go. Maybe having the house to herself would be good for her. I can't wait to ask her." Tooley said to himself. He looked at the digital clock next to his bed. It was nearly four o'clock.

"I had better get dinner in the oven and cook the green beans for us. It should be done just in time for Mom to come home!" Tooley predicted. He dashed to his cooking area and put the meatloaf in the appliance. He was proud of his capabilities. An hour would need to go by before the meal was complete.

Tooley plopped on the comfortable cloth recliner and rocked back and forth in anticipation that May would be back soon. He waited awhile and then turned on their thirty-two inch, semi-modern television. Channels were being flipped once he found the remote control. There was no satellite or cable service in the home but there were Tooley's local channels to choose from only. He flipped to his public television station and watched some Public Access, low budget shows. One was about the community school planning to add more computer storage rooms. The other show had somebody showing their audience how to lay tile.

Suddenly, the back door deadbolt clicked and May stepped herself inside the house from the back porch. She came into the kitchen with a book in her hand from work. It was about a new computer program that she was trying to learn.

She took another step and paused. "Something smells really good, honey! Oh, wow!" she could not get over how proud she was of her son.

"It's meatloaf, Mom-and a salad with a side of green beans!" Tooley announced and got up out of the chair and came over to his weary mother.

"Thank you, my child." May was tiredly appreciative.

"Go ahead, Mom, it needs to come out of the oven and then we'll eat!" Tooley went for the potholders hanging on a hook under the cabinet. He opened the oven and carefully pulled out the hot blue glass meatloaf dish. With his foot, he closed the door and set the dish on the nearby formica countertop. "Everything's ready, now come on, Mom." Tooley instructed. "Let's serve this up and take our drinks over to the dining room table in there."

"All right, son." May agreed and did what her child said by taking her portion over to the dining room.

They dined on their round pine table that seated about three or four on pine chairs.

"Oh, Tooley you really are a livesaver, kid." May complimented her Tooley. She smiled before taking another bite. "That tastes great, honey. The salad is so fresh!"

"Thanks, Mom." Tooley was happy. "Oh, I need to talk to you about something. Warren called me today and asked me to go with him to his little sister Amy's horse show up in Sedalia. If she wins, she'll be able to go to nationals in Albuquerque. Me and him will probably just catch her class and the rest of the rest of the time we'll hang out at the motel and swim and watch a movie on cable. What do you think?" inquired Tooley.

"Well, that sounds like a fun time for you guys. It's funny you talking about getting away for awhile, because I wanted to talk to you about something." May had Tooley in suspense.

"What's that?" Tooley was hoping that she was going to tell him something good.

"I have a paid vacation waiting for me from my job at the clinic and I feel like it's time for us to go somewhere for a couple of weeks, honey." May was trying to keep a straight face because she was so happy about that.

"When?" Tooley wondered.

"Starting after your graduation we need to leave. I am really burned out on my office work and we need to go on a vacation as soon as we can go in May. I'm sorry I didn't tell you sooner, but I had to find somebody who can replace me while we will be gone. It was no party, but I finally got Bev to take over for me. I apologize, son." May informed Tooley.

"That's okay, Mom." Tooley reassured her. "Where are we going to go?' he took a bite of salad.

"I've thought about some places." she answered after swallowing some iced tea and putting the glass down lightly on the table.

"Like where, Mom?" Tooley smiled a really big smile with one slightly crooked tooth.

"Well, I was thinking of a big city like New York City." said May.

"Really?" her son was amazed at the idea already.

"Yes, Tooley. I've been online at the office and got a map and lists of motels to stay at. And museums. We could visit the Metropolitan Museum of Modern Art, and the Museum of Natural History. I ordered some brochures for a lot of different places to chose from." May paused for a minute and ate her food.

"Gosh Mom. That sounds so great! I can't wait to call Warren and brag to him that I get to go with my Mom to New York City!" Tooley exclaimed.

"I know. It won't be cheap but my work will pay for it as long as I teach a class at a hospital there. It's in the Manhattan area." May sounded satisfied and was getting close to finishing her dinner.

"You'll see, Mom! I'll study extra hard for my finals!" Tooley said with his mouth full of lettuce.

"That's my sweet son! But all I ask is for you to do the best you can, baby." Tooley's kind mother stated while he shoveled the rest of his meal in his mouth. The silverware clinked against his white ceramic plate. Then he got up and cleared both places and took the dirty dishes back to the adjacent kitchen. He still had not stopped smiling as he practically ripped the telephone off of the wall to dial Warren's house.

"Hello?" a woman answered.

"Hi, Mrs. McNeal! Is Warren there?" Tooley asked Warren's mother.

"Oh hi, Tooley. Yes. Just a second." the phone receiver made a splatting sound in Tooley's ear. "Warren!" shouted Mrs. McNeal.

"Coming!" Warren said with concern. "Hello?"

"Hi, War. Guess where I'm going?" Tooley did not wait. "To New York City with my mother! She's taking two weeks off for vacation!" Tooley exclaimed.

"You'll be gone for two weeks?" Warren cried.

"Not for the whole two weeks, but I am not sure if it will be just for a week or what." Tooley guessed. "I'll find out more details when my Mom gets everything ready."

"At least send me a postcard." demanded Warren in a friendly tone of voice.

CHAPTER FOUR

Tooley's earth science teacher put two papers face down on each classmate's desk. They had taken the final exam three days ago and everyone in the class knew that this was their final test results. This result would make up a big percent-about thirty-of their last semester grade. Tooley breathed in the nervousness in the air of the classroom. It was so quiet that you could hear an eraser drop to the waxed floor.

"These are your grades on your final. I will grade on a curve. If you do better than most of your classmates, then you will get an A or a B. Most of you did well." informed Mr. Lake. All of his students seemed fairly happy with what was marked in red ink before their young eyes. Tooley gave himself a pat on the back after seeing his grade. It was an A -. Relief washed all over him as his grin got bigger and bigger. He thought to himself "One final down, and two to go." The clock above the chalkboard said ten minutes till ten in the morning. It had been Tooley's first class of the day all year. He would never have to come back to this room ever again.

"If you want to see the grade in here that you got, come up here and get in line to look it up." he paused. "It was a pleasure teaching this class to everybody. If anybody needs to talk to me, I'll be here. Have a nice summer." and with that he started showing kids their final grades. The bell buzzed and students packed up their papers and exited, talking excitedly as they went down the hall and to their lockers, most of them pleased with themselves.

It was down to just two more classes for Tooley to complete. He was just about ready to takle his typing final the next day. He was on the way there when Warren crept up on him in the hall. "How's it going, New Yorker?" he kidded.

"Great! I ended up with an A- on my earth science final. Now I'm headed for my last typing assignment. We are going to see how many words per minute I can do now compared to mid-quarter. Then our final is tomorrow. We'll have to type a form letter like people do in businesses." Tooley wanted his best friend to know.

"Sounds kind of easy." Warren assumed.

"Yeah, the form letters are okay but the hardest part for me is increasing my words per minute." Tooley said. He went on. "I need to earn some spending money for the trip. Mom told me if I could do that, it would pay for my souvenirs." Ginny next door needs help with her front and back yard work. I need to get that going after my last final." Tooley paused at his typing class door. "I have to go in here. See you soon."

"Bye. I'll ask my Mom if you can do our yard. I'll call you." Warren was late for his English IV class.

"Okay." Tooley answered as he chose a computer to sit at for his last assignment.

✳   ✳   ✳

"Tooley, I'm here." May had unlocked the front door and walked in their living room at about 5:00 p.m.

"Oh Hi, Mom!" Tooley came out of the cheery, cream colored kitchen. "How was work?"

"Pretty good. I've got some brochures to show you for our trip!" May was excited. She had not had a vacation, not taking a far away trip for at least ten years. "How was your final? You were a little nervous about it." May was hoping that he had done all right.

"Guess." Tooley challenged trying not to smile.

"Did you get an A?" May asked.

"I got an A- on the final and the same for the semester!" exclaimed Tooley.

"Oh! That's my little boy!" May cooed and rushed over to her son to hug him and to congratulate him.

"Thanks, Mom!" Tooley blushed. "All I need to do now is take my typing final tomorrow and then turn in my last history assignment and I am done with high school forever!" Tooley could start to feel some relief.

"That's sounding great, baby. I am so proud of you Tooley. Let me show you some brochures on the coffee table here and we'll start deciding what places we want to visit. Here." May laid down some brochures on the clean glass.

"read thesse over. There are some museums and a couple of hotel brochures." May instructed.

"Mom, I wanna go to the Statue of Liberty at least." Tooley requested.

"Yes. We will go there. I looked at where it is on my New York City map. Right near Battery Park." May assured her son.

"Are there a lot of parks in New York City?" Tooley thought out loud.

"Yes, I do believe there are gobs of parks there!" May answered. Tooley smiled goofily.

"I think I'll go to my desk and do my history assignment. My teacher is so cool. All my final is in there is answering questions over what we read of the last chapter. He's letting us use our books on the assignment, too!" Tooley scampered down the hall to his poster-covered bedroom door. He shut it and got to work on his history questions.

May happily got herself her iced tea and opened the refrigerator door to see about making some chicken for their last meal of the day. She was so pleased to know that Tooley was doing so well and was going to finally graduate. She knew that high school seemed to last a lifetime to Tooley as well as for herself.

*   *   *

"And that's all for today." Tooley's typewriting teacher commanded as the room became silent. The class had just finished their final test and everyone had finished printing them out. "Take your papers from the printers and put them on my desk up here." She pointed next to the apple that some nice pupil left. Tooley's printer was a little slow and was just then spitting out his final. It was a typed letter hopefully meeting all of the requirements of a good business letter. "Have an excellent summer." Mrs. Johnson looked relieved for her students and was hoping that they would all pass the final. Tooley was the last kid to hand in his paper.

"Have an excellent summer, too." he wished his teacher. "I'm going to New York City after graduation." Tooley beamed.

"Are you?" Mrs. Johnson asked. "All by yourself?"

"I'm going with my mother. We're going to see museums and parks. The Statue of Liberty will just be waiting for us!" Tooley declared.

Dinah Havens

"Well, tell your mother that I said you were an excellent student and it will show on your report card." complimented Mrs. Johnson. She winked at him.

"Thank you for everything, Mrs. Johnson. Maybe I'll visit your class sometime." Tooley grabbed onto his book bag. There was only one book in it. It was light compared to the beginning of the year.

"Just please remember to be safe." the teacher demanded passively.

"I will." Tooley said as he walked out of the computer-filled classroom. "Bye."

As Tooley walked down the hall, he knew that he would miss his teachers and his classmates. A lump formed in his throat and he nearly cried as he remembered to go drop off his history assignment at Mr. Humphrey's classroom. It was only a few rooms away so he wiped his eyes with his white t-shirt and entered the room with the globe sitting on the front table. There were stacks of textbooks laying on and around it. "Hi, Tooley, got your final assignment?" asked Mr. Humphrey, the funniest teacher in the whole school.

"Here it is." Tooley handed his teacher a couple of papers.

"What's this? A book report from the third grade?" Mr. Humphrey joked.

"Ha-ha, Mr. Humphrey." Tooley could tell he was joking and smiled. "I'm outta here." he informed his smart-mouthed teacher.

"Congratulations, sir." Mr. Humphrey put down Tooley's assignment on his cluttered desk and held out his hand for one of his best students to shake. Tooley firmly took his hand and a little shock got his. "Uh!" Tooley yelled in surprise as he quickly pulled his hand away. He could not believe that his teacher just did that old trick. He did not really have anything to say to Mr. Humphrey and dashed out of the room, leaving his textbook on the overpopulated front table.

"I had to just get out of there. Mr. Humphrey has a very dark side to him." Tooley thought to himself and walked to the end of the bus line. He let out a delighted sigh and could not wait to get home and call Warren.

As the sparsely filled Beachtown schoolbus braked at the curb with a squeak, it let out a deep breath. Tooley felt like he could do the same and got up out of his dark green seat. He went down the little usle quickly and told the large bus driver to stay cool this summer.

"I will, Tooley. Tell your mom to come play Bingo downtown sometime." the red-faced lady told her last student on her route.

"That sounds like fun!" out Tooley popped from his big yellow ride and he happily ran to his front door. He was excited to get inside to call Warren. Unlocking the bright brass lock, Tooley felt the need to use the bathroom first. He dashed to the hallway and closed the door behind him. Then the telephone in the kitchen started to ring.

"Okay, okay!" Tooley resented the impatient tone of the ringer. It did not give up, though. It had rung several times and Tooley was able to make it to the kitchen.

"Yes?" he nearly shouted.

"Hey, Tooley! You get done with your finals today?" Tooley smiled because it was Warren.

"Hi, buddy! Yeah, I think I did great, too. Mr. Humphrey is one sick man, though." Tooley said.

"Why? What did he do this time?" Warren had Mr. Humphrey too but was not in Tooley's class.

"He had a buzzer in his hand when I shook it. It scared the hell outta me! I am so glad we don't have to be the butt of his jokes anymore!" Tooley was so happy about it being the last day of school.

"What a dumbass." Warren retorted.

"He can be sometimes, but oh well. At least we are graduating." Tooley looked at the bright side.

"That's right, and I'll be doing that with honors." Warren was content.

"I think that's great! Because so will I!" Tooley paused. "Do you and your family have any plans for this summer?" he asked his best friend.

"I don't know yet. I don't think we'll be going to New York or anything, no. But I did get an early graduation present." Warren was just waiting to inform Tooley about the gift from his parents.

"What did you get?!" Tooley was loudly interested.

"A brand new digital cam –corder to record my graduation with! I mean, Mom can do that but it's all mine!" Warren exclaimed.

"Wow, man! You did earn it. We could have a lot of fun with that! We could shoot home movies with it or something!" Tooley cried.

"The battery is charging up right now!" Warren could not wait.

"How great is that?! I know you have worked so hard. You deserve it!" Tooley complimented.

"Yeah. I guess I do!" Warren agreed.

CHAPTER FIVE

Tooley's whole senior class threw their black caps up into the air. The whole auditorium was full of friends and family. Everybody was overjoyed. Tooley grasped his high school diploma and darted over to where his mother was sitting.

"Oh, son!" May's face was a little bit red as tears fell down.

"Mom!" Tooley hugged his mother tightly for a moment and then let go. "I'm so happy!"

"Oh, congratulations! Do you want to go and get some ice cream?" asked May as she sniffed. Just then, Warren came running up to them with a breathless smile.

"Congratulations!" he cheered, holding his camcorder up, the red light blinking on record. He captured Tooley and May holding up his well-earned diploma. "Look at my new present, guys!" Warren squinted.

"Hey, shut that thing off!" Tooley was a little bit self-conscious. "You got us, now turn it off." Tooley ordered, without a frown.

Warren did as he was told and pushed the stop button and cut off the power.

"Let's get some hot fudge sundaes downtown at Minnie's to celebrate. What do you say, Warren?" Tooley asked his happy friend.

"I need to tell my parents." Warren said.

"They could come, too." Tooley suggested."We could meet at Minnie's in fifteen minutes. Huh, Mom?" Tooley looked at May.

"Yes, boys. We can all meet there." she agreed. Some rainbow colored confetti fell on all three of them from a nearby group of students.

"Yay!" they were shouting. Tooley, May, and Warren paused to look over at them, smiling. Laughing, the group of students posed for a digital camera being held by a parent. It made a noise similar to an eagle's cry, only softer.

"Okay, Mom. Let's get out of here!" Tooley exclaimed, excited to never come back. Then, mother and son rapidly walked out of the loud auditorium, down a noisy hall, and out to the graduate-scattered parking lot. Some cars had been marked up with white shoe polish in words like "Just Graduated" and Class of 2008." May got in her Saturn and so did Tooley. They pulled out of there and rode down the lilac bush-lined street toward Minnie's downtown. They were not alone in their endeavor. Other relieved kids wanted to celebrate their accomplishments at Minnie's.

Arriving there in the back parking lot, May and Tooley got out of their car and walked to the front entrance, and went inside. It smelled delicious in there. They got pretty hungry just catching a whiff of barbequed meat and looked for a table big enough for six to include Warren's bigger family. The sign at Minnie's door had said to seat yourself. So they zeroed in on a table in the back. Luckily, no one had taken it, so they had a seat in it. They scoped the restaurant for Warren. In he walked with his family and his cam-corder within five minutes. He spotted his colleagues and came over to the table gesturing for his family to follow him.

"Over here, Warren!" Tooley directed. "Let's have some ice cream!"

Everyone had a seat, a little tired from the festivities.

"Separate checks?" a waiter asked, holding a small pad of paper.

"We'll take care of the ticket. All of this on one ticket, please." Mr. McNeal informed everyone. "Hot fudge sundaes for everybody here."

"That'll be six hot fudge sundaes." the young waiter said to himself, and he headed toward the busy kitchen.

*　　*　　*

"Twenty, forty, and ten makes fifty." Ginny could have very well been a teller at a bank at one time. "You have no idea how hard it would have been for me to do all of what you did for me." she shook her head at how little she could do anymore. "Thank you for saving me from all of that yard work, sweetie!" Ginny was relieved.

"I appreciate the extra money. I'm going to need it on my New York trip. Souvenirs aren't very cheap and the fifty dollars will help me a lot. Thank you." Tooley was grateful.

"New York? I'm sorry I couldn't give you more! I hear it is very expensive to live in New York City. I've never been to that place. You two deserve a break seeing that you graduated. So proud I am of you! You must be really smart." Ginny admired. "Tell your mother that I am happy for you guys."

"I will. I'll write you a cool postcard or something. I know your address. Well, we'll be leaving tomorrow on our way to St. Louis to catch an airplane for New York City!" Tooley looked a little droll with excitement. "See ya when we get back, Ginny!" he headed out her front door and walked calmly back to his residence. "Such a nice kid." Ginny giggled.

Tooley's mother was doing the last load of laundry.

"Hi, Mom! Guess what? Ginny gave me fifty dollars for mowing, raking, planting some petunias, and walking Tiny on his leash." Tooley bragged, a little smug.

"I think that's great, baby!" May said, a little in a hurry. She was excitedly getting ready for the busy schedule that they had to abide by all day tomorrow.

"Make sure you pack enough for a week at least. You won't need a swimwuit because there's no pool at our hotel, okay?" she told her son.

"Okay. I guess swimming won't be on our list of things to do anyhow." and with that, Tooley went to his bedroom to fatten up his suitcase.

The next morning was crisp and clear in Beachtown with only a few feathery clouds in the sky. It was time to head toward St. Louis. May loaded the suit-cases in the trunk of her car and Tooley grabbed his spending money.

"We got any maps of St. Louis?" Tooley wondered.

"Look in the back seat and find the Missouri page. You can tell me what hi-ways we need to use as we go. It should take us about three hours to get there." said May as she looked over her shoulder to back out of their driveway.

As they escaped Beachtown, Tooley felt so glad to leave for awhile. He enjoyed being the passenger, looking at the last neighborhoods and the fresh new green of the countryside. He could see the river in the distance. It was sparkling like the sequins on a blue-green homecoming gown. Time seemed to go by slower now, after rushing around to get ready. May was ready to notice all of the road signs so as to not get lost. She turned the car stereo on not too loud so Tooley could concentrate on some navigation. The alternative music she had in the compact disc player was good for staying interested and awake.

"Take this exit, Mom, you'll need to switch to another highway." Tooley said an hour and a half later.

May turned off the music for awhile so she could focus on how the road would take her to the next route. "Okay, I see." May said as she got on the sure path. She needed not stop to fill her gas tank because she had filled it already.

"Good job, mother! You're a professional!" Tooley kindly encouraged.

"Thanks, baby. We'll be at the airport in no time." May was glad to say. As the mother and son team approached the St. Louis area, the traffic grew thicker. Tooley summoned the St. Louis metropolitan area map and explained that they should go around the city to get to its airport.

"Hey, Mom, see the arch from here?" Tooley was staring to the east.

"Oh yeah, I do." said May, trying to get a glance of it while she was driving. "It's so bright and beautiful! I wish we had time to stop there. Our flight leaves in only a couple of hours, so we better be moving along." she said regretfully.

CHAPTER SIX

The airport was bustling with people rushing to their appropriate terminals and gates. Luggage was dragged along with wheels and Tooley and May had to take that walkable "escalator" to get to their desk. Then they headed to some waiting seats and May talked to the airline clerk to sign in.

"New York City, wow!" the young clerk was imagining being at that destination.

"Yeah, for vacation with my boy." May winked.

"That sounds like so much excitement! I hope you have fun! Just show me your ticket when you board! Have a wonderful flight and thank you!" schpeiled the clerk.

"Thanks." May went to sit down and wait with Tooley. They waited an hour like most airlines want one to. Tooley listened to a battery operated radio with earpieces. He found one good station that played a variety of rock music, his favorite. Both of their stomachs were growling, but lunch came with the flight. They could not wait.

"Now boarding!" the airline employee yelled into her microphone after time went by.

"That's us!" Tooley jumped up and grabbed his carry-on bag. May got up with hers and followed her son through the hall.

Once they found their seats in first class, Tooley sat down and could not believe how comfortable he was. His mother was so happy, he could tell.

"Wow, Tooley, we've never flown first class before." May declared, looking around and noticing flight attendants checking people in their seats to be sure they all had their seat belts on. Babies screaming in a very shrill tone were sitting in the row across the aisle from them. An adolescent with low patience turned around in a seat in front of them and very grouchily yelled "Shut up!" He could not have been older then seventeen. He was annoyed. May and Tooley looked at eachother and tried not to crack up in laughter. Instead, they smiled for quite awhile.

Finally, a flight attendant with a dorky tie gave May and Tooley complimentary drinks. Tooley wanted, requested, and received a large Coke. He was so comfortable and loved the flight. May had a screwdriver and then another one.

"I feel so relaxed, Tools. (May called her son Tools on occasion.) I can't wait for the city! This is great." she basked in her observation. "I see the clouds! Tooley, look at how we are in the clouds. That's beautiful!" May marveled.

"Yeah, Mom. It's cool in a weird way." Tooley said as he glanced out the rounded rectangular airplane window. He yawned. "I'm sleepy. I'm going to try and nap before they serve lunch." he told May.

"All right." May agreed, being tired also.

When lunch got around to them in a stainless steel cart, they offered tri-tip roast and vegetables. It was chef quality food. May and Tooley accepted the platters with interest.

*　　*　　*

As their steady flight reached New York City, the pilot told everybody to look out to the left side of the plane to view the Statue of Liberty. You could hear half of the passengers give a slow "Wow…" at the same time.

"Hey, Mom! Look! The Statue of Liberty!" Tooley pointed down on his window. May observed the mighty oxidized creation.

"Yeah…Hey Tooley, you're right. The Statue of Liberty…" May trailed off as she tried to stare at it for as long as the plane speed would allowed.

"Want to go first thing?" Tooley asked in a very quick way.

"Sure, kid. Let's do that!" May declared as she leaned back in her upright positioned seat. The airline crew had their final say as everyone was getting ready to land.

"Ding, ding…"

At LAGuardia airport, the pace was busy and fast as is usual for an airport in a big city. May and her son approached the automatic doors to the outside with their new luggage.

May had thought ahead and found some really nice black leather bags for a great price on a home shoppers network.

Taxi cabs swarmed the entryway waiting for their next customers. Some got occupied rapidly. May held up her hand with her arm. "Taxi." she yelled, remembering people in the movies doing just that. She had spotted a lady driver with curlers in her hair.. "Come on, Tools." Tooley grabbed their belongings.

May got in the back seat and said "I need to use your trunk, please."

The woman turned around and said "Hi, welcome to the city! I'm Lucy."

"Oh. I'm May and my son, Tooley, is the cute guy with me." she introduced while Tooley was already getting in the back seat next to his mother.

"My, my! Where are you from?" she asked before she started driving. She had noticed Tooley's bulging biceps. Her cab smelled nice and fresh, as if it had come from a dealership.

"Beachtown, Missouri." two voices answered the friendly lady at the same time.

"Oh! That's the Midwest! I hear that you all get an awful lot of tornadoes!" she cried, not being able to imagine herself getting sucked in by one.

"Yes, we do. And we just had to take a vacation for once in our lives. Right, son?" May explained, looking to her child.

"Yeah. I just graduated from high school." Tooley said.

"How exciting for you! What a great feeling it must be!" Lucy was genuinely happy for Tooley. She paused. "So, now. Where would you like me to take you in The Big Apple?" she smiled, getting down to her job.

"Eighty-first and Columbus, please ma'am." May told the red-lipped Lucy.

"All right. Is that where your hotel is?" Lucy needed more information.

"Yes. It's called the Hotel Celsior. Do you know where it's at?" May asked.

"Mhmhum. That's a great place to stay! It's easy on your purse, too." Lucy was now looking in her rear-view mirror at her customers. She knew exactly where to drop them off. "I can hear your southern dialect. You two sure are from Missouri." she said, as she got past some airport traffic.

"Yeah." May yawned

"You'll love it here! You'll never run out of things to do." she was enthusiastic.

"Neat!" Tooley was already looking at building after building going by during their trek. They were in the city now. It was going to be a pleasant culture chock, coming to their hotel in a taxi.

Tooley noticed townhouse after townhouse with people's front stoops right up close to the public sidewalks. There were people wearing colorful clothes; some looked like they immigrated from other countries to America. All kinds of people conglomerated the streets. A lot of people looked busy, and some looked like they were having a very hard time keeping up with their lives. Some people were smiling and having a fun time occupied with their own worlds.

"Here we go in the tunnel to get to Manhattan, babies!" Lucy cried. They ventured into the tunnel all lit up with lights. The passengers felt enveloped in concrete safety as their taxi seemed to whiz by all of the comforting lights. They were leaving Queens and going to be entering Manhattan. Daylight on the other side of the tunnel appeared and they had bypassed the East River completely.

"Did we go across a river?" May wanted to know in an impressed sort of way.

"We crossed the East River just now." Lucy said. "Watch out for the jellyfish this year!"

Manhattan had an impressive skyline. It had the Empire State building and the beautiful Chrysler building that looked like that style of car. It was very cute in a tall fashion. Also, it was full of parks. The trees of Central Park were an intense prolific green against the tombstone skyscrapers.

"There is the Museum of Natural History. It is right by your hotel. They have dinosaur bones on exhibit all of the time. I think your son will love it, May." said Lucy as she stopped in front of their destination. "And Central Park is just down the street on eighty-first and Eighth Avenue. Here we are, now I hope your trip will be wonderful!" Lucy let her travelers out of the cab.

"Bye, Lucy!" May said and paid Lucy. "You've been so helpful!" She was getting tired as Tooley took their bags to the curb. They looked at the canopy over the entrance to where they were going to check in. "All right, son. Let's check in and get to our room." May wanted to get her shoes off of her flat feet.

*　　*　　*

Room 333 was presented to the two hungry and exhausted tourists. The owner, Becky, opened the door for them revealing a comfortable hotel room with cable television.

"I hope that you have a pleasant stay." she smiled sweetly. "Let me know if you need anything at all. We have the Cozy Café downstairs." she offered as she did to all of her guests, and went down the hall dressed in a khaki skirt and a cool white blouse.

"Phew." May sighed and looked out of the big picture window at the breathtaking view.

"Oh, Tooley. Look! Look at all of the skyscrapers! It's so unbelieveable!" she cried as Tooley witnessed what she was seeing for the first time in their lives.

Hey. Yeah, Mom! Oh wow!" he was speechless for about five minutes. Where do we go first?!" Tooley was overwhelmed with delight.

"Let's go get something to munch on after we get ready to go out." May suggested and went into the restroom to clean up. Tooley did not protest and sat down on the bed next to the phone. There was a pamphlet on the outdated nightstand that said room service was twenty dollars plus the bill amount. "Geez." he said as he tried to fathom how expensive that would be. Their hotel, however, was considered affordable compared to the "nicer" ones in New York City. Tooley decided that the room was comfortable, clean, and nice enough. It was a little bit old though, like it was built in the nineteen twenties with doorknobs on the doors that looked like crystals.

Tooley again went over to the life just outside the window. It was getting dark now, and lights were starting to show up brighter and brighter on buildings. Some skyscrapers had neon lights outlining them and some had light bulbs glowing up close and in the distance. Some of their windows were lit up and you could see in a little. Most of them were offices. Some windows were dark. However, Tooley was truly mesmerized. He could not imagine all of the wild evenings that New York's citizens might experience. Suddenly, the gray restroom door to the bathroom opened and May looked like she felt better now in an oversized t-shirt and jeans. "Do you want to go over to Rockerfeller Center where NBC does their shows and eat something? she asked Tooley, who snapped out of his thoughts.

"Yes, I am starving!" he cried.

"Let's go!" May exclaimed. Then both of them darted to the painted door and walked down the hall to the elevators. May was putting her purse strap over her shoulder as they did this.

Once outside, May said "It's this way. We'll have to walk south down the length of Central Park West to get there." So they walked and walked past groups and groups of people. A lot of them were speaking a different language other than English. Tooley tried to pick up on Spanish as some Americans passed them on the somewhat crowded sidewalk. He understood a little bit of what they were saying, but the Spanish was spoken so rapidly that his thoughts seemed to scatter. There were some boutiques along the way with t-shirts and stylish jewelry displayed out on the sidewalk. Pottery shops were doing this too, with their various styles of ceramic examples. Tooley thought that a lot of things were nifty. He remembered his yardwork money and had to stop at one boutique to get a punk rocker black leather bracelet with silver studs. May bought a classic t-shirt with the I (heart) New York printed in bold letters on it.

As they made it towards Rockerfeller Center, they passed Radio City Music Hall in all of its redness.May remembered that she heard that the famous Rockettes did their performances there. Their legs were about to give out as they turned the corner and sat down at a table on the wintertime ice skating rink. It looked totally different in the summertime at Rockerfeller Center. The ice skating rink was retired for the summer. Instead, tables with umbrellas and chairs that looked like tasteful patio furniture were employed.

"Cheeseburgers are fifteen dollars here! Jesus Christ!" May was looking at the menu.

"What will we order?" Tooley asked nicely.

"Go ahead and get a cheeseburger and fries, I suppose. Everything else costs too much money for me." May grumbled. She was a little disenchanted. "Manhattan must cost a fortune to live in." she said wearily.

"Okay, Mom. Hey, I noticed that St. Patrick's Cathedral is back around that corner. Want to check it out?" asked Tooley, holding the map that May got from her office computer.

"Sure. That'll be two cheeseburgers, fries, and waters, please." May ordered to the smiling waiter who had crept up on them during their conversation.

"Yes, ma'am." he replied as a group of pigeons gathered toward the table.

"We really need to take a cab back to the hotel from there. I cannot walk anymore." May announced to Tooley. After about ten minutes, they savored their meal. A group of Amish people walked by near them in their 1800s-era clothes and in their seriousness.

"Imagine coming all of the way to New York City to see people from Missouri!" Tooley said softly. May noticed that too, and smiled.

"Yeah. Let's go see if we want to convert to Catholicism." Tooley joked, and off they ventured.

*　　*　　*

"Tooley, wake up, honey." May coaxed the next morning. She needed to tell her son that today is the day that she teaches her class at the New York Hospital.

"What's up, Mom?" Tooley questioned.

"I have to go to my class now. I'll be back in a few hours." she made clear to Tooley.

"Okay." Tooley complied and noticed that it was ten o'clock in the morning. "I might go to the Museum of Natural History while you're gone but I'll be back here in time to meet you." Tooley was just itching to go there. He loved anything that had to do with studying about nature.

"Okay, Tools. Tell me what you learned from there when I get back. Goodbye." she whispered. With that, May gave her son a kiss on the forehead before she went out of the door. Tooley was overwhelmed with a sense of freedom. He was going to have fun going to the museum all on his own.

May went out of the Hotel Celsior and hailed a cab.

"New York Hospital, please." May requested as she got inside.

"All right." the driver said in an English accent.

"Where are you from?" May asked innocently.

"I'm from London." he said. "Where are you from?" he asked in return.

"Beachtown, Missouri. It's a very small town right by the Mississippi River." May explained.

"Oh- a small town girl." the driver teased, yet became thoughtful. "Like Tom Sawyer!" he remembered reading Mark Twain.

"Yeah, I came here on vacation, but I teach a class at the hospital so I can have it paid for me and my son. He's probably on his way to the Museum of Natural History by now. He's so excited to come here to your city." May said happily. The cab sped up for once after being in a bumper to bumper crunch.

"And… here we are!" the man said in a tone of finality. "Have a good class!" he wished his former passenger.

"Thank you kind sir." May replied and paid for the friendly transport.

The hospital was a tall, noble establishment. Cabs were up by the front entrance. People with all kinds of situations were coming in and out of the place. A man with a broken leg was successfully balancing himself on his crutches. He smiled at May and let her walk to the doors in front of him. "Thanks." she said, feeling a little guilty that she was in good health.

On May went to the lobby with the main elevators waiting for their next victims. She had been told that her class was in room 301. Up she went in the elevator along with a couple holding a newborn baby in its car seat. It smiled and gurgled.

"What a sweet baby you have!" May complimented the new parents.

"Isn't he, though?" the mother asked confidentally, almost rudely, in a flat tone of voice. May could tell that she was nervous. She was probably just worried about her baby for some reason. May did not want to talk to them anymore and walked out onto the third floor toward her class. This time, she was ordered to instruct a diabetes class. She wondered how many people would show up.

She paused at room 301 and looked inside. The caged clock on the wall said 11:00 sharp. She was glad she was on time, and went on up to the podium. Her teaching notes would be stretched out in front of her. There were about twenty desks in the room and posters about diabetes were on the wall. One said "Diabetes is no joke." May had to laugh anyhow. A shelf with pamphlets and medical supplies including needles stood next to the chalkboard. Someone had written a healthy example of a meal plan in yellow chalk. Windows lined the wall and were open, allowing for any breeze that would be kind enough to make itself known to anybody who might be ready for it.

"Hi, teach!" someone said all of a sudden. It was a rather heavy man in a blue t-shirt. He seemed a little pushy acting and sat in the front row.

"Hi. What's your…" May started to ask but was interrupted.

"Are you the teacher for the diabetes class?" he asked.

"Yes." May sighed. A few other people walked in with notebooks and pens. She gave them a smile. A minute went by and another small group of people came into the sparsely populated room. They may or may not have been together. May wanted to get started as the clock's long black arms approached five minutes after eleven.

"Okay everyone. Get a sheet of paper for some notes. We're going to answer any questions you have about…" May was rudely interrupted once again. The man in the blue shirt was turned around in his seat asking the others behind him for a piece of paper. May went on.

"You need to be prepared for all that diabetes requires. Asking questions about it is a very good way to begin that journey. Who has a question?" May asked her class.

"Yes." said the man in the blue shirt and went on. "Do I need to not eat fruit because it has sugar?" he asked while he looked down at the scribbles he was making loudly.

"No, not completely, uh, what's your name?" May was innocently curious to know.

"Okay." the guy said quickly.

"Okay…" May said in an annoyed and confused tone of voice.

"Who else?" May tried to get on with helping some others. Before she knew it, she was being attacked by that son-of-a-bitch. He had her on the cold floor, holding her down so hard that when she struggled to get free, she still could not get away. "Help!" she cried. "Help!"

It took more than one of the other students to get the fat creep off of their nice teacher.

"You want to tell me I can't eat anymore?" he yelled as he broke loose of the students and went over to the shelf and grabbed some hypodermic needles. He ran back over to May as she was getting up and stabbed her in the face with about three of them. "Uh!" May yelled and backed forcefully away from the man in the blue shirt who would not even tell his name to the class. She fell against the window sill yet could not stop in time and fell backwards out of the window!

CHAPTER SEVEN

May was frantically bracing herself for the fall with her hands behind her to hopefully break her drop to whatever surface fate would dictate. It happened so rapidly that all May could utter was "Ahhh!"

She fell on a pedestrian who was walking on that sidewalk and crushed her before she met the concrete, shattering her arms as they protected her back from being broken. There was still one needle stuck in her shocked face as she fainted right there. A man who looked to be a nurse came over to May and did not want to move her but instead called someone on a cell phone to come down immediately.

The injured lady pedestrian was mostly terrified and seemed to have a sprained ankle when the male nurse tuned in to see what state she was in.

"Oh my God, oh my God!" the lady whined as she was trying to make sense of just what had taken place.

"Breathe, breathe, ma'am…good. Very good. Someone will be here any second to help you. Try to be calm. You're okay." the puzzled nurse said, trying to be calm himself. He hid his fear really well and started to take charge.

He went over to May and took the hypodermic out of her face. She was moving in and out of consciousness, barely aware of the pain of her broken arms. A group of medics carefully transferred her and the other lady to stretchers and resolutely rushed them into the hospital's emergency room. The crowd that had gathered near the two women watched in hope that they would be all right. All of May's now former students were competing for a view out of that opening that would forever change things for Tooley.

✳   ✳   ✳

Tooley had walked over to the Museum of Natural History to see what exhibit was there. He was inside the huge building, admiring and enjoying a dinosaur bones exhibit. The bones on display towered over mankind. The boy felt so small standing next to the prehistoric archives. He loved the Jurassic period skeleton of a once carnivorous dinosaur. "How did these creatures actually survive here on earth?" Tooley quietly asked himself. Then he went over to check the tour schedule. It was for a special slide show about his very question, only it did not start for another couple of hours.

"I'll go back to the hotel's Cozy Café and have lunch." thought Tooley. He turned to go out the big doors to the outside pleasantness of a spring day in Manhattan. Central Park greeted Tooley with sounds of music being played. People were playing orchestral music. A group of violin players, he could see a small crowd of people in the park where the music was. To Tooley, it sounded a little bit like a piece by Beethoven that his mom would listen to on some mornings while getting ready for work. He smiled as he thought about how much he loved his mother's taste in music. She liked all kinds, but Tooley thought that her selections were very interesting.

He walked to Columbus and eighty-first street and

entered the hotel's tallness. The Cozy Café smelled of steak and spices and of bread and vegetables. He was so hungry that he could order a meal and dessert. Seating himself on a stool in front of a long counter, the lady, wearing a white fan piece on her old head, asked Tooley "What would you like today, bud?"

"Please bring me a top sirloin cooked medium, a small Caesar salad, a roll, and I'll have a piece of your beautiful thin mint pie, please! I'm famished!" he declared.

"I think I can help you with that, dear! You're a growing boy! How many girlfriends do you have?" she asked in a complimentary way. Tooley was flattered. "None right now, but maybe I've been asked out a couple of times." he was blushing.

"Order up!" she crowed to the cooks behind the open window.

Tooley could not wait until he could get his mom to go with him to the slideshow. He needed to get back up to the room soon to meet her. He wondered how she was getting along in a strange city. A few moments went by before his meal was presented to him.

"Oh boy! Thanks, ma'am!" he said gratefully, and chomped down his juicy and tender spiced steak. He savoured it as he got ready for his pie. Still, he was hungry, and ate the dessert feverishly.

"Put it on my room account, please." Tooley ordered, feeling very grown up. His mother told him that he could do that as long as he did not order the most expensive thing on the menu there at Cozy Café.

He went down to the elevator and got up to their floor. He took the dim hallway to their room. Using his key card, he opened the door and noticed that the phone on the nightstand had a blinking red light on it. Tooley came a little closer and observed that it meant that they had a message waiting for him. He hoped it was for him and picked up the receiver to reach the front desk and ask what the message was and who it was for.

"Operator I have a message on the phone here in room 333. Can you tell me the message please?" Tooley was good with people on the phone.

"Yes, for Tooley. That's a cute name! And it says for you to go to the New York Hospital's room 814 and find your mother. She's had an accident."

"What happened to my mother?" Tooley asked wildly but the operator had no further clues.

"I would suggest taking a cab over there and go to her room. It's number 814. I'm sorry, son." the operator was sympathetic.

"Thank you. I will." Tooley said softly and hung up the phone. He was starting to feel lost but he knew that he needed to use logic to get to May. He hurried out of the room and out of the hotel. He hailed a cab and told the driver to step on it and get to New York Hospital as fast as he could.

"Okay, kid." said the bashful driver. "I hope you are all right." he said while looking quickly in his rear view mirror at the very horrified boy.

"I am, it's just that something's happened to my mother and I need to be in her room to see if she's okay!" his voice was increasingly louder and fearful.

"I'll have you there in no time." the driver had a sort of Brooklyn dialect.

"Thank you." Tooley's voice was soft. The black and yellow vehicle pulled up to the hospital's front entrance fairly quickly and Tooley dashed out after handing the fare over to the guy for services rendered. The driver looked on as Tooley sprinted through the doors.

"Poor kid. I pray for a miracle for them." the driver pondered before picking up an old man.

*   *   *

Up in room 814, chaos could be a good description of what the young son witnessed before him. Nurses were making things more comfortable for May while her casted arms were being placed in front of her as she was in a bed that was all propped up. Other nurses were putting I Vs in other places on her body for hydration and for pain medication. There was a band-aid on her face and doctors were there discussing the MRI that had just been done to check out her concussion that she aquired having fallen out of a window from the third floor. Tooley ran over to his mother and kissed her on her face.

"Mom! Are you going to be okay? What happened?" Tooley had so many questions. May looked like she barely could see or hear her son but nodded her head up and down slightly to acknowledge that she saw him.

"Can somebody tell me what happened to my mother?" Tooley cried out to anybody who was listening. The nurse who first called the paramedics heard him loud and clear.

"Are you her son?" he responded.

"Yes, I'm Tooley."

"Sorry to meet you like this. I'm Eli. I regret to say that I saw your mother fall down on the sidewalk from a window on the third floor. She landed partly on a pedestrian but mainly she met the sidewalk. Her arms were shattered and she's got a concussion. They are going to be checking for internal bleeding. A few ribs were broken as well." he hated to inform the scared teenager.

"Fell out of a window?" Tooley could not believe what he was hearing.

"Yes, son. I found out that she was the teacher for a diabetes class on the third floor and the hospital knew her phone number where you guys are staying. I left the message for you." Eli explained.

"Oh. Thank you." Tooley had to sit down in the only chair in the room. He was deep in confusion.

"She had been attacked by a very sick man while she was teaching. Some of the students had called the police and that is how I found that out." Eli went on to say.

"That son-of-a-bitch!" Tooley's heart rate escalated. "What will I do now?"

"Stay here with her for as long as you need to. It looks like your mother… is it May? Eli interrupted himself.

"Yes."

"It looks like your mother will be staying longer than you guys thought. Maybe you should continue your stay at your hotel and visit for now. Then, when your time at the hotel is over, you will be more than welcome to stay here at the New York Hospital for however long you want. They might move her to a different room in a few days, but they'll let you sleep there and use the bathroom. Her purse and belongings are being kept safe here, too. But you do what you want. Here is my cell phone number. Call me if you need anything at all."

"All right, Eli. I think I'll just walk back to my hotel room and I'll check on Mom soon." he said and lowered his head. He left May's room and headed for the Hotel Celcior.

All of a sudden, the city seemed so different. There were people everywhere. Tooley did not think that anything was great anymore. There was nothing anyone could do to ease his mind. Eli seemed nice, but Tooley felt like he was incomplete without May and he had the loneliest feeling come over him. Depressed, he no longer wanted to rush to the tour at the Museum of Natural History. He took his time and had a few people pass him from behind on the sidewalk. He hated them for that. And then he became angry.

"What makes you all better than me? Being in a hurry sure doesn't!" Tooley yelled at no particular individual. He hoped that they all would be late. He began to believe that city people were rude and all he wanted was for his mother to be there with him. He wondered who that man was and why he had done that to her.

Then the boy noticed St. Patrick's Cathedral. It sort of stood out from the other buildings with its graveyard all fenced in. Tooley wondered if the people buried there were important or something. The cathedral stood with its stained glass catching the evening sunlight.

"This place is really old." Tooley noted. He went on inside to pray for his mother and the pedestrian that she had fallen on. It was pretty dark in there except for the candlelight coming from behind the altar. Some people were sitting in the beautiful pews scattered about, lost in thought. Some of them got up to light a candle to represent their prayers. Tooley liked this idea. He quietly prayed for his mother. "Dear God, please watch over my sweet mother as she heals. She is everything to me and I hope you listen to my prayer. Not only do I need her, a lot of others need her, too. She is a teacher and if she isn't around, people won't learn what they need to. I love her so much. And God, please be with the person on the sidewalk that got hurt. See to it that that man does not hurt anybody else. In Jesus' name, Amen." Tooley had his eyes closed and hoped for the best. He felt somewhat better and went to the glittery altar. He took two simple white candles and lit them ceremoniously with eachother. May's young son let the flames burn in front of him and wished that their energy would get through to the higher power that everyone had so much faith in.

Turning away, Tooley felt like getting to the hotel to try to calm down. It was going to be tough to do that. He really felt that if he knew what that psycho looked like and if he saw his stupid face, he would kill him in the most painful way that he knew. Heavy would be the blanket in store.

CHAPTER EIGHT

The next day, Tooley woke up after having a nightmare. In it, he had written a letter to his mother about how he loved her very much and was going to find the bastard who attacked her. The letter came back to Tooley with "Return to Sender" stamped on it in a purple neon color. He wrote more letters but they kept on being sent back to him. Finally, Tooley cried and woke up.

"What the hell?" he had just realized that he had had a very bad dream. As he got out of bed, he saw the view out of the window. "Great." he thought as he remembered what happened the day before and still could not believe that terrible message that he got. "If only this was not happening." he wished as he tried to get cleaned up. This new day was not a welcome one for May's son.

Eventually, Tooley decided to call nurse Eli to check on any progress that might have been made for his mother. He took out the card with the cell phone number and punched it into the hotel phone on the nightstand. It rang about three times.

"Hello?" answered Eli.

"Eli?" Tooley asked even though he recognized Eli's voice.

"Yes, Tooley?" he asked. His caller i.d. made him into a psychic.

"Hi." Tooley said in a quiet voice.

"Hi, kid. What's on your mind today?"

"Is my mom awake yet?" Tooley needed to know.

"Well, I checked in on her this morning and it looks like they are managing to keep her awake. They were testing her memory and she asked where you were. She had a pretty bad fall, but I think she would like to see you and could talk to you for awhile. Come on over to the hospital." Eli suggested in a cheerful and inviting voice.

"Okay…Hey Eli, do you know if they caught the bastard?" Tooley was anxious to find out, naturally.

"I was hoping that they would, but all I know is that police were questioning the rest of the students that were in her class yesterday." said Eli. "I think they must have given good descriptions of him."

"Damn. Well, I guess it's going to take some time." Tooley paused. "I'll be up soon after I get something to eat. Is it the same room number?" Tooley asked.

"Yes. Room 814. I probably will be busy working, but you can contact me anytime. I'll be checking on her every day for you." Eli was trying to be as helpful to Tooley as he could be.

"All right. And thank you for everything, Eli." Tooley wanted Eli to know that he was thankful for all of his care.

After his brunch of fish sticks and cheese sticks, Tooley left Cozy Café and hurried as fast as his feet would allow toward the hospital. Tooley hated this situation so much that he felt that he might lose his mind. His trust for people was hanging in the balance and it was about to fall down over his head. He ran and raced down the sidewalks, ignoring all of the sights and sounds. He almost got hit by a taxi cab.

"Beep! Beep!" it went, and the Middle Eastern looking driver looked scary with a big frown and a turban.

"Watch it, asshole!" he yelled, and spit out of his window as the brakes squeaked. All Tooley could do was run faster as he gave that cab driver the longest finger on his right hand.

✳   ✳   ✳

"'Tools, is that you?" questioned May, a little slowly, as her son came into her full vision. She felt the need to hug him with her arms, but could not move. Frustrated, she cried out in pain.

"Ah, Mom. How are you?" Tooley could only guess what her answer to that would be.

"Oh, I'm alive…I suppose." was her only reply. She swallowed hard, the only sign that she was in physical anguish. The only improvement made in her recovery was that the Band-Aid on her face was no longer necessary.

"I was so worried about you!" Tooley was relieved to see that his mother was responding to him.

"I'm so sorry to see you like this." Tooley started to get tears in his eyes. "I want to find the person who did this to you." he said in a sad, yet determined vocalization.

"Oh, my boy! Are you staying at the hotel?" she asked as a nurse came in to give her some lunch.

"Yes, but it's just not the same without you." he said.

"Mmmm." May relished her food as she was being spoon fed.

"There ya go." said the young nurse gently and patiently. Tooley was overwhelmed with what he was seeing. He could not stop his tears and got a tissue from May's bedside table.

"I'm going to stay at Celsior for the rest of our reservation time." he informed his transformed mother. I'll come every day and be with you for as long as I can and then I'll stay in your room until they make us go home." Tooley repeated

nurse Eli's suggestion. May smiled at her son and k
she was lucky to be alive even though she was not very happy
about suddenly having broken arms and ribs. She had Tooley
push a button next to her bed and asked the nurse's station
for some pain medicine.

Their reply was "Right away."

*   *   *

A week had gone by, and Tooley wondered when they
would be going home. He was so disappointed with the trip,
and felt that it had been some kind of evil trick placed on
him by an ever invisible devil. He wanted to actually see the
source of his devestation. He thought that it was a real wimp,
not being brave enough to show itself in some kind of physical
form. Because it forced them to miss out on so many good
times, Tooley had fallen into a depression deeper than the
ocean. He needed some answers to his prayers and felt a little
bit like his faith in God was being tested. It was never going
to be the same again for him. He felt that his stay at the hotel
was a three hundred and sixty degree waste and he knew that
he would always wonder what they could have done together
in New York City. Now he would have to take their bags to
the hospital like it was some kind of campsite for ones who
awaited on either heaven or answers. They would have to stay
there until the doctors and nurses said that it was okay for
May to go back to Missouri. The saddened child started to
feel like he lost a huge bet in Las Vegas and now had to just
turn around and go home without any winnings.

His yardwork money was desentegrating and he counted
it to see what remained.

"Only eighteen dollars." he groaned to himself, rolling
his eyes. Yet, another taxi was hailed while he held one bag
and had to keep the other on the gritty concrete. He was not

looking forward to staying at the hospital for an unknown amount of time. It almost made him feel as homeless as a snail without a shell.

He climbed into the cab and it took him to his sorry destination. Without a word, he paid his driver and took the luggage up to where May was.

Upon entering room 814, Tooley noticed right away that it was empty. Tooley saw somebody mopping the floor over by the window.

"Hi." the housekeeper said, still wearing a look of concentration, not looking up.

"Can you tell me where May Reynolds is?" Tooley asked and then checked to see if he had the right room. It was truly room 814.

"Um, you need to go to the nurse's station to the left once you turn around. They will be able to tell you." the housekeeping employee said, finally looking up at Tooley.

"Thanks." Tooley said, and followed the housekeeper's directions. He reached the nurse's station.

"I need to find my mother, she was in 814, and now nobody is there." Tooley said in a louder, more confident way. The nurses looked up from their computers.

"She was moved to room 500, sweetie." the nurse behind the counter said calmly. "Take the elevators over there and just go to floor five and room 500 should be just on your left." her painted fingernail pointed in the direction that she was talking about.

"Okay. Thank you." Tooley said politely and fast, tapping the countertop once firmly. He charged towards the elevators like a bull charges at its matador. He really did not think that he could deal with any more people and tried to get to room 500 just as soon as he could. He started feeling panicked and power walked to May's new room. He thanked God that nobody had gotten in his way.

"Mom!" he said as soon as he saw her. She was asleep and a nurse was washing her hands in a little sink in the corner of the room. "That wasn't so bad, was it?" he was asking, even though May was in her healing slumber. Then he left the room without anything else to say.

Tooley went over to his favorite lady and pulled up a chair. He did not want to wake the woman and decided to just lay in the empty bed next to her.

CHAPTER NINE

"Warren?" Tooley had just dialed his best friend's phone number.

"Tooley! How is New York City?" he inquired innocently.

"I'm not in New York City. I'm back in Beachtown." Tooley answered grumpily.

"Well, how was your trip?" Warren asked happily, not knowing what had happened.

"My mom fell out of a third story window at the New York Hospital." the disgruntled boy filled Warren in.

"Uh…what?!" he could not believe what he was hearing.

"Warren… my mother was attacked while teaching her health class." was all Tooley wanted to explain. He just wanted to let Warren know what had taken place in Manhattan.

"Oh my God! Tooley, are you at home? Where is your mother now?" Warren could have been an interviewer for Time magazine.

"We are both at home. Mom's got a visiting nurse until her broken arms and ribs get better. She has to have pain medication and other pills. She has a concussion and is lucky to be alive…A pedestrian broke her fall somewhat and now she is going to recover at home. I guess I'll be feeding her and keeping watch over her. After she heals, she's going to need physical therapy. I just thought you should know." he explained, being surprisingly calm.

"Gosh- Tooley, I am so very sorry." Warren paused. "When can we visit?" he asked gently.

"I guess just come over in the next couple of days." Tooley ordered.

"Okay, Tooley Anything you want. Let me know if I can help you guys." Warren offered.

"Thanks. I just might." Tooley grumbled and hung up the kitchen phone. Then he went over to his mother's hospital bed that had been set up in their living room.

Beachtown's only community hospital's nurses had come and settled May in. They told them that they would send a nurse later that evening to start May's home care. Tooley was tired and anxious at the same time. He had never had that feeling before.

Tooley was very unsure about what would progress that summer. There were so many things that he wanted to do but now he really had no desire to do them. He wondered how long this would last. He called up nurse Eli and told him that he would be helping take care of his mother. Eli could tell that Tooley was depressed. He suggested that Tooley go to a support group as soon as possible and told him how to get ahold of one in his area. Tooley really did not feel like being near people, but wrote down some phone numbers just in case he changed his mind. He thanked Eli and they wished each other well.

Tooley noticed that May went to sleep while watching Oprah Winfrey and went over to her. She looked so sweet that she seemed like a little child. Tooley pulled her comforter up to her neck and kissed her on her forehead. Her face was healed from the needles being stuck there by that maniac. He coul not wait to ask her what he looked like. Angry, he went to his bedroom and punched his red punching bag until he was no longer able to punch it anymore.

*　　*　　*

"This is important, youngster." the older lady nurse commanded. "While I cannot be here all of the time, there are some things you should know about caring for your mother." she was getting ready to explain.

"Like what?" Tooley was trying his best to listen.

"I will be here in the morning and at night. My job is to make this wonderful patient as comfortable as possible. I must bathe her every morning, cook for her, feed her, give her the medications that she's been prescribed, and to help her stay cleaned up. You must observe how I do these things tonight so that you can help her when I'm gone." the nurse answered the boy. "My name's Melanie, by the way. And your name is Tooley, right?"

"Right. And my mom is May." Tooley said politely although he was feeling overwhelmed.

Tooley learned that he was to give May her medications at noon. He watched her drain the bedpan and flush the contents down the toilet. Keeping the house clean as well as cooking meals was important. As far as feeding her, he thought that it looked easy enough. He knew to feed her nutritiously; and he wrote all of the emergency phone numbers down. Watching over his mother was going to have to happen for the next two months. Then the nurse told Tooley that she was sure he could do it and that she would be back in the morning.

*　　*　　*

One morning, after several weeks of cooking, cleaning, wiping, economizing, and shopping-Tooley was growing more frusterated and felt he needed to go to a support group but did not have time nor the gas money to go.

In the mailbox outside, Tooley discovered some unusual looking envelopes address to May. He opened the mail anyhow. Inside was a bill for his mother's stay at the hospital. The total amount owed was burned in Tooley's memory forever. He nearly fell over right there on his very own front porch. It came to a price that Tooley was very shocked by. In that moment, his mouth went dry and he felt extremely queasy. He wondered how someone would be expected to pay such an amount just for having an accident.

Going back inside, he slapped the bills down on their dining room table. "I must at least show Mom these. I hope it doesn't send her into a bad state…No, I think I'll wait until she's better before I show her bills like these." and with that, Tooley thought that decision would serve his near future better. He was reeling, and just did not know what to think. The intelligent boy was thinking that he could show the nurse and see what she thought about it.

Sometime in the next few minutes, Melanie herself pulled into the gravel driveway, the small rocks making a crumbling sound on her tires. Tooley saw her through the blinds out the living room window. He decided to greet her at the front door and to let her inside in order for her to do her magic.

"Hi, Tooley! How's my best helper?" she asked nicely.

"I'm not so sure how I am today, honestly." answered Tooley, looking at the floor.

"What's bothering you?" she seemed to care about what the problem was.

"I got something in the mail that I cannot show Mom until she's got her life back." Tooley said, getting down to the reason for his stress.

"What on earth is it?" the concerned lady questioned.

"Look, it's some hospital bills." Tooley went for the dining room table and grabbed the documents. "See? This is how much Mom owes that place."

When the nurse had seen the numbers in the highlighted box, she stared at May's son in disbelief, then she shook her head.

"I think you have a good idea not to show her this until later on in her recovery. Do you know if she had medical insurance?" she asked.

"I don't know. I guess I could ask her on that later, too." Tooley was not looking ahead to doing that, the expression on his young face in a frown.

"She will be able to go over that with you later. Maybe they can arrange a payment plan for her. I know that they can work with you on something like that." she half smiled at Tooley and said "Don't you worry about it for now. You have been doing such an excellent job running things and keeping up your mother's care. You're just a kid, so just wait another month or so to bring it to her attention." the nurse was trying to reassure Tooley that he had nothing to worry about now.

Then the nurse set to work and replentished May's needs for the morning. Tooley pulled some strawberries out of the refrigerator and gave some to the experienced doctor's assistant to give to May. Then he sat down by them and ate breakfast. May was contently eating having been made comfortable by the medications that the nurse administered right before the meal.

May was cleaned up by Melanie afterward and she felt better. She liked the no rinse shampoo and was just as clean as if she had just gotten out of the shower by herself. May told her nurse friend goodbye and that she would see her that evening.

"Goodbye, May." the woman left Tooley and May in their living room. "She's so great at her job." May remarked, and looked at Tooley. "Is everything okay, dear?"

"Uh, yeah, I'm fine." Tooley lied. He was still upset from that bill in their mailbox.

"Thank you, son, for being here for me. I cannot begin to tell you how much I love you for that." May said, feeling bad about her son having to wait on her hand and foot when Melanie was gone.

"You're welcome." Tooley replied and was trying to cheer up. "I think I'll go outside for some fresh air, okay?" Tooley asked, heading for the door.

"Okay." May said as her arms throbbed through the pain medication.

Once outdoors, Tiny, the neighbor lady's dog, came to its fence in its back yard.

"Hey, Tiny! Hi!" Tooley greeted the puppy before it started barking at him.

Tooley walked on by, too nervous to stop and pet the sweet creature. He did not feel like faking being happy when he was not. "Sorry, Tiny." Tooley thought to himself, and went on down the gravel road toward nowhere. The dog kept on barking at him, noticing that something was wrong. He kicked up some gravel rocks out of anger "That bastard! Now I'm having to be Mom's nursemaid just because he lost control. What an asshole. I wish he could compensate me with the money that it would have cost had Mom paid some nurse's aid to do what I'm doing. And I have to do a lot of the work for no pay from him? If only I could get to him. I'd rip his testicles out through his throat!" Tooley cried out loud. "Although-all the money in the world wouldn't make up for my mom's and my mental pain. What's it called? Pain and suffering?" Tooley was trying to unload on an invisible person. He knew that he was just talking to himself, but he did not care. "I should be the one to be paid! Why do all the nurses and doctors get to be paid but not me? I could practically be a nurse by now! Is it written all over my face that I enjoy working for free? I don't think so!" and having said all of that, Tooley turned around and went back home.

CHAPTER TEN

The hot month of July went by slower than an old car with a flat tire, but it finally came to an end. Tooley had decided that today was the day to show May her hospital bill. Her arms and ribs had healed successfully. Now a physical therapist was coming to their address three times a week for the next few weeks.

Tooley had already thought about getting some kind of job to help pay the bills that might find their way into the mailbox. He saw a "Help Wanted" ad in the Beachtown Bugle. They needed workers at Beachtown Slaughterhouse just outside Beachtown right near the Mississippi River. That was the only ad for work in the classified section.

Sitting there on his bed, he glanced over at the clock on his wall. It said 12:15 p.m. on it in digital numbers. "Okay, I'll go show her these bills now." he said to himself and reluctantly walked into the kitchen where his mother was standing at the counter. "I need to show you something, Mom."

"What's that?" May looked over her shoulder.

"I can't believe I have to make you look at these." Tooley said to his mother, squeezing his eyes shut as he handed her the dreaded papers.

"What?" May gasped as she unfolded her bill. She glanced at it and laughed, not really grasping the monstrous calculation. Then she looked at it again and her lovely smile vanished. She now found out how much her stay at the hospital had cost. May turned around and cried "How ridiculous!" as she stared in exasperation out into space. All Tooley could do was stand there and look stupid. At least that is how he felt. Stupid for not being by his mother's side when that superdork freaked out and hurt her.

"I wanted to get a job to help you with the payments." he offered.

"Oh, no! That is not really how much I owe! Is it?" May was dumbfounded. "What did you say, sweetie?" she was trying desperately to stay calm.

"I wanted you to know that I will get a job to help with the bills." Tooley said.

"Oh, that's really sweet! But you don't have to." May did not want her baby to have to work. She hoped that she would not need him to. Yet she added "That would be nice though, because I don't have health insurance."as she glanced at Tooley's t-shirt. It had a big bear on it.

"Really?" Tooley was not liking what he just heard his mother say.

"Yes. It's true. I haven't any, even though I work at that medical clinic. You'd think they would have given me some. I don't know. I'll call them and ask if they'll help pay some of it since I got hurt doing a class for them." May concluded.

"Okay. But my offer still stands." Tooley said firmly.

"All right." May sighed. "Thanks, Tools."

"I love you." Tooley doted.

"I love you, too." May answered. "Let's have some lunch." her face was a bit peaked.

*   *   *

"It smells really bad." Tooley said to himself as he pulled into the slaughterhouse parking lot. He had just dropped May off at her work. This was the place where Tooley wanted to get a job application form to fill out. It was obvious where the main office was. The biggest facade on the massive compound was located in the center of it. Tooley got out of the car and hurried towards the cold, grey iron doors.

"Okay, Tooley. You've got a job here at Beachtown Slaughterhouse. I'll have Jose` show you the routine today. You can pick up your schedule after your shift. We'll give you some aprons and you'll need to get you some supportive shoes. You'll be reimbursed for them later." said an older, balding man with a typical southern dialect. "Bring your lunch to work and you get two seven minute breaks during the shift." he announced and left the office for a minute. He returned with a Mexican kid of seventeen. "Jose`, this is… um…" the man looked closely at his desk. "Tooley? Is that it?" he asked.

"Yes…Nice to meet you, Jose`!" Tooley said enthusiastically, yet nervously. Jose` only nodded his head towards Tooley, not smiling. He seemed a little bit wise for seventeen, but Tooley thought little of it and braced himself to learn his new job.

"My name is Larry and I will be your boss. If you need to tell me something, tell me. We start at $6.00 per hour. You get raises for evey month of work you do. Jose`, take it away." Tooley's new boss reqested." And-congratulations!"

Tooley thanked Larry and followed the kid down a bulletin board-filled hallway. There was another set of iron doors, only these had square shaped windows at the top of them. Jose` opened them up, revealing Tooley's future work area.

"Here, we slaughter thousands of chickens and cows for their meat every day." Jose` pointed at the football field-sized space full of fluorescent lighted work lines. Tooley spied a line of plucked chickens hanging single file on a conveyor belt up towards the ceiling. They were waiting to be quartered after the USDA veterinarians were supposed to inspect them.

"Here is your station where you hang each chicken up on the line by the neck." Jose` grabbed one out of where the live chickens are put at the very beginning of the streamlined slaughter process. They looked confused and unhappy, squawking as if they knew what would become of them.

Then he stuck one chicken by its neck in a little shackle on the conveyor in a very rapid fashion. "You have to do this very quickly because the shackles move at a certain speed on the conveyor belt. That's about one chicken per two seconds when you get really good at it." Jose` explained, the expression on his young face showing no emotion. "You'll need to wear these protective gloves and an an apron." Jose` handed the articles over to his trainee. "And remember to get some good, supportive work shoes. We pay you back for them." His English was not perfect.

"Okay." Tooley was trying to remember everything that he was being told to do.

"Any questions?" Jose` challenged, almost smiling but not quite.

"No, not right now." Tooley replied.

"Okay, you be punching out this time card at the office in about eight hours from now." Jose` stated and handed it to Tooley.

"Can I work part time?" Tooley asked, because that is what he had in mind.

"Ha!" Jose` cried sarcastically.

"What?" Tooley was showing his innocence. He had no idea how things worked at a slaughterhouse.

"No such thing as part time. Full time or no time at all." Jose` laid down the law.

"All right. Full time." Tooley repeated him to show that he was listening. "I need this job."

"Very good! Now you start doing what I showed you, and you be okay." Jose` directed.

"Okay. It was nice meeting you!" Tooley smiled and said. Shaking his head, Jose simply went out the iron doors and hoped Tooley would be successful at his new job.

*   *   *

"Full time." echoed in Tooley's brain as he was hanging up live chickens hand over fist for a progressing hour. His feet were starting to ache because he needed better shoes. The gloves that he was wearing did not protect him from when the chickens were squirming and struggling to stay off of the conveyor belt. They were so terrified that they scratched Tooley's arms. With its claws, one chicken made a very long scratch all the way along his forearm up to his sleeve. "Damn!" Tooley shouted as he realized that tomorrow he would have to bring a long-sleeved shirt with him. It had only been one hour and he already was getting scratches. He wondered if there was possibly a nurse around somewhere. He looked around for Jose` for a moment, but he was not anywhere nearby. He glanced further down the line at another worker. She was making sure that things were running okay. The conveyor was not slowing down for Tooley and she saw this.

"Get back to work! There's no time to just stand there like a dummy!" the older lady yelled.

His arms stinging, Tooley got back to work with the chickens. He did not understand what the precious rush was for. "This is how fast I am for now. If they don't like it, then fine!" Tooley was thinking as the next chicken he grabbed pecked him in the arm. His first reflex was to drop it on the sludgy floor. "Ow!" the new worker cried. The chicken was smartly making its way back out from where it came from, toward the big overhead door. Tooley laughed, feeling some kind of justice for that one bird. "Oh, well." he mumbled, hoping that his arm would stop throbbing, and got back into the tornadic pace of his job station. The August heat created sweaty grime all over his brow. The grumpy older lady was busy at her station, making sure that her birds were being killed by a big, circular blade. The ones that the blade missed would go on to be quartered alive. Sometimes the blade was dull, the speed of the workline not stopping for it to properly be sharpened.

Tooley had not seen this up close and was just busy trying to keep up with his overindustrialized position. He did not seem to have any time to notice, but his nice tan colored loafers were turning grayish-green with filth. Chickens commonly would let out droppings right there as afraid as they were to be hung up in that huge closet known as Beachtown Slaughterhouse.

"Ah choo!" Tooley was getting a little bit allergic from all of the feathers going by his nose.

"Hey!" he yelled toward the lady working nearby. "Stop the line!"

The lady heard him and rushed toward Tooley, frowning.

"The line isn't stopped unless we are repairing it! What's the problem, kid?" she crowed.

"I have to use the bathroom, please!" the youngster pleaded.

"You'll have to wait until your break." the woman snapped. "Now, back to work!"

"But I-" Tooley was cut off.

"You want me to go to the boss?" she threatened.

"No, I-" Tooley could not believe this testy female.

"Good." she interrupted again and walked away.

"Who the hell is she?" Tooley asked himself, glancing at his watch. His break was not for another couple of hours.

"Screw this." he said, and decided to go right there in his pants. "Ah choo!"

*   *   *

Tooley pulled into the clinic parking lot to pick his mother up from work. Out the door she came, smiling at her son.

"Hey, baby!" she got in the car and asked "How was your first day at work?"

"All right, I guess." Tooley said tiredly.

"I guess?" May prodded.

"My supervisor is a bitch from outer space, but Jose` was nice enough." Tooley answered.

"Jose`?" May echoed.

"Yeah, he's the one who showed me how to do my job. He says I need some supportive shoes and they'll pay me back for them." Tooley was not looking forward to having to go shopping.

"My feet are killing me! I have to stand up all day and I only get two seven minute breaks!" Tooley complained.

"Poor baby! Let's go downtown and get you some shoes." May said, trying to be sympathetic.

"Okay, Mom. But I'm really tired. Let's just hurry up." whined Tooley. Away they drove, headed for the shoe store.

*   *   *

The next morning, Tooley dropped his mother off at her work and headed for his job at the slaughterhouse. He was glad that his mother had bought him some new shoes, but he really did not want to hear it from that supervisor lady today. He arrived and went inside the gates of hell.

"Hello, Jose`." Tooley greeted his latest acquaintance. "How are you?"

"Okay. Aren't you a little early?" he observed.

"Yeah. Here's my receipt for the shoes I got. Hey, what's the lady's name who works down the line from me?" Tooley asked.

"That's Cathy." Jose` told him.

"Oh. She's not very nice to me." Tooley commented.

"It's her job to make sure the line keep going." Jose` explained without feeling one bit sorry for Tooley.

"Okay. Well, I guess I'll get on my shift." Tooley sensed coldness amongst them and did not want to hang around. He went into the work area and to his station. Cathy was at her station, doing something to the blade that she worked with every day. The line was stopped so she could work on it. All Tooley could do was wait for her to turn the line back on. All of a sudden, the blade came on, sucking Cathy's long gray-brown hair into its rotation. It did not stop there. Before Tooley knew it, he saw her face get sucked into it. The blade then ground it all up as if it were stuck in a blender.

"Someone, turn off the air knife! Now!" Tooley yelled. There was nobody around. "Jose`! Get over here!" Tooley ran to the office. "Jose`!"

"What's going on?" Larry asked.

"Stop the line! Cathy just got sucked into her blade! Someone must have turned it on while she was working on it! Stop the line!" Tooley was shaking in horror. Larry dashed to a control box and shut off the line. He then ran out to Cathy's station. Tooley was no less than half a second behind him.

"Cathy!" Tooley screamed. Her body lay on the floor, drenched in blood and headless.

"Oh no!" Tooley shouted and looked to Larry, who was speechless. The blade was covered in blood and brains. Tooley could not believe what had just happened, much less the very sight in front of them.

"Oh, God!" Larry cried. "Cathy!"

"She was just working on it! Someone turned it on before she was finished! Didn't they see her?" Tooley wanted to know, his heart pounding at almost two hundred miles an hour.

"You keep your nose out of this!" Larry snapped. "She will be replaced! You take the rest of the day off and come tomorrow." Larry then called the on-site paramedics. "There's been an accident."

Tooley ran out of the place trying to understand why Larry said what he had said. Tooley started to sob uncontrollably as he got in the car. He was not sure if he could drive, yet started the engine and sped off. He tried to stay calm and not to panic as the stinky countryside flew past the windows. The sooner he could get home, the better. He wanted to call Warren and tell him what he had witnessed at his second day at work.

CHAPTER ELEVEN

Arriving at the most comfortable place in the planet, Tooley made a run for his front door. He was going to call Warren. He was all alone in the house and it sounded dreadful. "At least it's cool in here. That piece of inferno is a hotbox. Now I can inhale in my own area." he thought very nervously.

Grabbing the phone on the wall, Tooley frantically dialed up his best friend. "Come on, come on! Warren, answer!" the kid yelled, in tears all of the while.

"Hello?" answered a girl.

"Amy, I need to talk to your brother right now." Tooley tried to hold it together to spare the girl any worry, yet, he failed a little bit.

"Anything the matter?" Amy asked, knowing that she was hearing Tooley's voice.

"Uh, just let me speak to Warren, please." Tooley had lowered his voice, trying to get what he needed.

"Okay, Tooley." Amy complied and dropped the receiver. "Warren, Tooley really needs to talk to you!" she shouted as if Warren was in the other room.

"Coming!" Warren could be heard exclaiming, and picked up the phone. "Yes, Tooley-boy?" he asked, not having any idea what he was about to hear.

"There was an accident at work, Warren. A horrible one." Tooley was still shaking. "I mean, I do not even want to say anything that will bring you down, but, at work, I looked up and saw a fellow worker get killed by a big blade!" he was hoping that it had not actually happened, but he knew that indeed it had.

"Oh my gosh! That's unbelieveable! You saw this?" Warren was concerned about his best friend. And worried.

"Yes, I did. And I am not going back. I'll have to find another job! How am I going to be okay? I'm just trying to help with my mom's medical bills!" Tooley protested.

"Okay, Tooley. Please try and calm down. I am happy that you got the job. I'm not happy that this happened, but it was an accident." his friend coaxed.

"You should have heard my boss, though. It was as if he didn't even care! He said that she could just be replaced!" tears fell down Tooley's angry face. "I hate it there!"

"I don't blame you. You are so brave, Tooley. And I'm sorry about New York City, too. I keep asking myself why that happened to you guys. And then this-it has really made me angry. Even my parents and sister are pissed. I wish I could take away all of this." and Warren threw his basketball against his living room wall. It bounced off of the television and landed on the couch table, breaking television and landed on the couch table, breaking some precious trinkets of his mother and sister's. "Dammit!" he yelled. Tooley heard the crash on his end.

"I'm going to get another job, you just wait and hide!" Tooley yelled back. "I'll call you later." he said, hoping that he would not be stuck working in that house of horror.

"I guess I'll never know who accidentally turned the line back on." Tooley said with great wonder. He tried to just stop freaking out and to quit pondering on his more than bad day from Hades. He had a grinding headache and took a few aspirin, yet he wished that they could also calm him down. Then he remembered that there was a six pack in the refrigerator and dashed towards it. He grabbed a couple and went to his room to listen to some music on the radio. His mother would not be home for another couple of hours.

Tooley was lost in the music on the only rock and roll station available in Beachtown. He was starting to get a buzz and then he realized that the newspaper was in the other room. He went to go get it, and plopped down on the couch to read the section where job offers were.

"Free horse manure." laughed Tooley, as he thumbed through the black and white pages. "Jobs." Tooley spotted the same ad for the slaughterhouse and one other ad. "Doctor needed at clinic." he read aloud. "Great. Now I have to wait longer." Tooley snapped to himself. "Oh, well." he surled, and wadded up his second can of Paapst Blue Ribbon. Stumbling to the trash can, he pitched the can and went for another cold beverage.

The day wore on as the sun spat upon the roofs in the little neighborhood like bacon in a frying pan. The air conditioner was working overtime and there was no sign of the rain or storms that were desperately needed. Tooley stayed indoors and went to his room again and fell asleep on his bed. The music was still blaring throughout the house.

"Tooley, I'm home!" May shouted as she came through the back door. She heard Tooley's radio and ran to his bedroom.

She turned it off as she noticed her boy unconscious on the bed with a beer sitting almost empty on his desktop. "What's up, son?" she questioned and sat on the edge of his bed. "Honey?" she summoned, and pulled on his foot.

"Wha?!" Tooley screamed briefly, then noticed his mother. "What time is it?" he felt like he was late for work and had to get up immediately.

"It's five till four. I got a ride home early and was going to call you at work." she explained. "Are you all right?"

"No, not really." her son whined. "I had a really hard day. And I'm not sure if they would have approved of you calling me. They're stingy about that kind of thing." Tooley did not feel like sharing with his mother what he had witnessed. He just did not feel like repeating himself. He decided to tell her later if he could just stay calm.

"Okay, then." May agreed and should have known that work at a slaughterhouse would be disappointing for her high school graduate. "Hey, Tools... she trailed off, noticing Tooley's frown. "My work said that they would pay ten percent of my medical bill. That doesn't exactly amount to much, but I guess it would help."

"That's all? It was their stupid classroom that got us into this damned situation!" Tooley shouted, scaring May a little bit. She could tell that he was very depressed.

"If only we hadn't taken that trip! I wish I could take it all back now! But, Tools! I don't know what to do now that we're back, honey. We just have to take things one day and then take them the next day. Each day will just have to be a step forward." May said as best as she could. She was starting to cry, regretting that Tooley had to work because of the accident. She ran out of the room so that her son could not see her cry. May also did not want to explain herself. She decided to figure out what to make for dinner. There was not much there in the kitchen. The budget for the week was spent on groceries already, but she figured that she could choose something acceptable.

*   *   *

The next day chased the night away, like a viscious guard dog scaring an unsuspecting jogger. The morning was an inescapable lukewarm sauna, and it was going to be much steamier later on. Birds as well as outdoor pets were anticipating another unforgiving oven of an August day. They were being as active as possible before the smothering heat came on in the afternoon. They were secretly wishing that the extremely hot sun would not shine too hard this time, while Tooley's alarm clock approached seven- thirty. It started to scream and cry harshly, and he rolled over onto the floor.

"Uh…!" Tooley moaned when he landed there. His mouth retained the taste of last night's beer, and a hint of its odor had occupied his nostrils. "Oh God…" Tooley had sort of a headache as well. He had nausea in his stomach as a result. Anxiety was almost instantaneous at that next moment as the teenager realized that he must go back to work again. "I hope I can get a different job to do there. I don't want to go back to that same spot. There must be a way to ask Larry without him getting angry." Tooley pondered vocally. "There's no way that I won't throw up just looking at Cathy's old place on the line." Tooley visualized yesterday's mishap and burst into tears. He absolutely hated what his tender young mind played back. All he could do was hope that a new job would magically open up for him.

"Tools, are you up? Come on, kid. You need to drop me off by eight-thirty. Get up!" May said firmly at her brave boy's door.

"Tooley did not care what she was squawking about. All he could hear were muffled requests piling up outside his closed door like accumulating snow. "'Kay!" he managed to answer, and dragged his seemingly heavy feet across his bedroom floor.

Waking up was painful for Tooley. He desired so to get back into his slumber, back into bed. That was the only place that the old child felt safe and comfortable. He opened up the blurry door and faced a breakfast of oatmeal and pear slices.

There were no words exchanged during the drive to May's work except when she was getting out of the car.

"Tell them that ten percent isn't jack!"

"I know, Tools." May said and let out a sigh. "Try to have an okay day."

"Love you, Mom." Tooley left her with that and drove away, hoping that he could achieve that.

He arrived at work a little bit early so that he could talk to his boss, Larry. He was really nervous about doing that, being a new worker and everything. Nevertheless, he took a huge breath and forced himself into Larry's office.

"Good morning, son." Larry greeted Tooley cheerfully enough.

"Good morning. Could I ask you something, sir?" Tooley asked.

"What is it?" Larry looked at Tooley innocently, as if nothing had ever gone wrong a day in his life.

"Would it be possible for me to work at a different job? I don't think I can look at my station the same way ever again because of what happened to Cathy yesterday." he explained, his hands getting sweaty with fear.

"If I let you do something else, I'll have to take the time to find someone to do the job you're doing now. Look, I know that wasn't the best thing for you to see…is it Tooley?" asked the man.

"Yes. Tooley." the boy stated curtly.

"Tooley. I like that name. Are you named after anyone?" he asked, trying to take up as much time as he could before he had to say what he was going to insist on.

"My grandfather was a carpenter, but now he's gone." Tooley explained, wondering if Larry even cared.

"That's wonderful." he laughed. "Wonderful. Now, kid, I could put you on something else if you could just hang onto the work you've been doing for just another week or so. Then I could find a replacement for you. It's hard enough that I have to get someone to do Cathy's job. Jose` may have to fill her place for awhile. Could you do that, Tooley?" Larry might as well could have been telling him.

"Gosh, I-well...I guess I could try." Tooley offered, although very disappointed.

"There is no try, child. Either you do it or you don't." Larry said sharply. "Now, go on and I'll send Jose` to come talk to you whenever there is someone to help us."

"Okay." Tooley said quietly, looking to the floor for comfort. He felt like his life was getting to be a tumultuous series of disappointments. Asking himself if this existence was ever meant to be his own, Tooley went to his gloriless location to go back to work. Jose` was at Cathy's place at the air knife. "Hi, Tooley." he greeted Tooley without looking up.

"Hi, Jose`." Tooley said and paused. He wondered if it bothered him to be working where someone was brutally ground up like hamburger meat. Yet, Tooley did not really even want to ask about it. He knew that it probably did upset him. He was not even eighteen years old. It had to have left a scar in his mind.

Jose` was pretty good at his job sending chickens through to the knife to have their heads chopped off after their "baths" in the scalding tank. That water was so hot that it literally scalded the feathers off of them while still alive.

Tooley set to work by grabbing more frightened chickens and hanging them up in the same repetitive fashion over and over again. "Surely I won't be working here for long." Tooley thought to himself, longing for a break. It was getting hot already, and he felt that he needed some water. "Jose`!" he cried. "I need something to drink! I'm thirsty over here!" he was blinking his eyes to keep the sweat out of them.

"Next time bring some with you in bottles or jugs." Jose` replied unsympathetically and kept working without stopping. "Wait until the break."

*   *   *

Tooley threw the newspaper down on the kitchen counter after eating his breakfast. "There's still no work around here in this stupid town!" he yelled in exacerbation and stomped out the back door, leaving his mother on her day off to sit and stare in disbelief. She was hoping that some kind of job would come along so that her son might be happier. At the mere suggestion of Tooley going to a psychologist, he blew up at her last night saying it was the world who needed a therapist; not him. And the sad part of it was that she agreed. She felt completely paralyzed with the uncertainty of not knowing what would become of her youthful son's spirit. She vowed to keep an eye out for any opportunity her son might have to work somewhere else.

Tooley ventured on to his job in the family car. He had the phone number that Eli the nurse had given him in order to check up with the NYPD. The boy needed to see if they had caught up with the psychopath who shattered their lives. He was not even going to expect that they had tried to look for him. For if he assumed that the cageworthy imp was now locked up, he would be in for a let down from somewhere as cold as the North Pole. Tooley did not have a warm enough coat for that blast of air. Yet, he planned on calling the number after his long day.

"Tooley, now the boss has a new job for you." Jose` startled Tooley as he was just arriving inside the area of streamlined production.

"Really?" Tooley was not expecting to change jobs for a couple of more days. "Where at?" he asked.

"Over in the other building." the young supervisor blurted out.

"Okay… will you show me?" asked Tooley.

"I'll find someone who will over there." Jose` answered. "Follow me."

Tooley walked behind the kid and went through a couple of sets of double doors. To Tooley's dismay, there was another work area similar to where they just came from, only the product was beef. There were more people working on the line and they were working fast. "I'll introduce you to Roberta, who will show you your job. Here she is." Jose` said as they walked toward an older lady of maybe about fifty years old. "Roberta, this is Tooley-the new kid who will be doing what you are doing. You, in turn, will be at another job. Please show Tooley everything about your job." Jose` ordered and said "If there are questions, you may page me from this phone." he handed Tooley a black cellular phone. "Keep it charged up at the offices." Jose` then turned and walked away, not smiling as usual.

Tooley raised his eyebrows and looked at Roberta. She had her straight, dark brown hair up in a bun, which was not a bad idea. Then Tooley noticed her hands. They appeared to belong to an eighty-year old, not a fifty-year old. Her fingers were curled in bunches and looked very arthritic. It made him curious to know how they got that way.

"Tooley, right?" she asked.

"Yes. And you're Roberta?" he asked and held out his hand to shake hers. She did not hold hers out, though. "What happened to your hands?"

"It's the result of all the repetitious work I've done here for about five years now. Okay. First, you should always bring a jug of water with you before you get to work. They won't let you get any while working." she winked.

"Yes, I brought some. I left it at my old station. I'll get it real fast." Tooley ran to get it as if it was a pot of gold. He returned in a moment. While he sat down his big beverage, Roberta went on.

"This is a line where we get cows ready for slaughter. Your place is to knock them unconscious before sending them to the sticker, who then hoists them and slits their throats." Roberta explained and then handed Tooley his knocking device. "You use this to blow each one in between their eyes on the forehead. You need to move quickly because one will be ready for you to do right after you get done with the last one."

"All right. Let me try one." Tooley was a little anxious. There was a cow waiting in the knock box, ready for its turn. Tooley then went up to the brown and white animal and used his "gun" to get the cow unconscious, right between its eyes. It seemed to have worked. "Good. Just try to keep up a steady pace." Roberta then left him to find his own way to do just that.

Someone was driving cattle up next to where Tooley was. They let the animals in the box, and Tooley set to work. He kept thinking about hurrying and tried very hard to knock them as precisely as he could so he would not be stuck trying to get it right. That was a wise thought, but he noticed that he only had a few seconds to be precise, and the next cow was always being put to be next. It pressured Tooley to let a few animals go to the sticker (where they are supposed to die) conscious.

Some of the cows had to be knocked with the captive bolt device more than two or three times. Tooley could barely keep up when that happened, so if it took more blows than that, he had no choice but to let some conscious cows go through. He did not feel good about it, and was going to find Roberta on his next break.

As he did the best that he could on his first day, Tooley glanced over at the sticker. He was hoisting the cows up to be killed. Some were mooing in fear. The sticker was going just as fast as he could, too and Tooley noticed that the guy was not able to kill every animal. Some cows were going to be skinned and butchered while they were still alive and conscious. He knew that he could not observe that for very long. He could not slow things down, apparently. All he was able to do was think that this great line speed was wrong. He was ashamed that his knocking gun was not doing the job every time.

The day grew hotter for the workers and Tooley was glad that he had listenend to Jose` about bringing jugs of water. Still, the teenager longed to take his break at that moment. He could not do that for another couple of hours. Tooley wished that he could just run outside to catch a much needed breeze in the sunlight. Instead, he was forced to stay right in the same frustrating position.

"Boom." Tooley heard someone or something fall near the sticker. It was the sound of the sticker falling to the manure-covered floor. He had just been kicked down by a terrified cow who was trying to struggle free of the shackle she was being put on. It did not succeed in doing that, yet the worker that it had kicked now lay on the dirty floor.

"You okay?" asked Tooley, noticing that the man's face was red and that he was getting more and more angry. Before Tooley knew, the guy jumped up and grabbed an electric prod shoved it clean up the unsuspecting cow's behind. Tooley could hear it zapping the animal for about fifteen seconds. "Moo!"

"Take that, heifer!" the sticker cried in intense frustration.

"Uh…" Tooley responded, surprised. He turned away and pretended that he did not see the occurrence. He just hoped and prayed to himself that he himself would not lose it that badly. He felt bad for that man. It was obvious that he was just trying to make a living, and he ran the risk that at any second, he could get hurt. It seemed like he was having a hard time getting through his day. It was like watching a really bad episode of Jerry Springer, and one could not change the channel, much less turn off the television.

*   *   *

"Roberta, are you sure my gun works right? I'm having to use it three times at least for one cow sometimes." Tooley asked his coworker on his much anticipated break. They were standing outside; Roberta was having a cigarette. She held it with her curly fingers, and it looked more challenging than it was.

"Well, the voltage needs to be higher in them, but it was turned down so now it is not uncommon for the animals to not really go to the sticker unconscious. They are supposed to be, yet you can only knock so many properly as fast as they want you to go." she explained.

"So I noticed. You know, I wish the line could be slowed down somehow so that I could do my job right. I feel bad sending cows through as awake as Speedy Gonzales on coffee." Tooley laughed. "And maybe the voltage should be turned up stronger."

"I have complained about that before. They don't listen to anyone who works here. In fact, they once told me that I was lucky that I didn't get fired for complaining. They don't care. They don't allow unions. The line goes their speed only.

It makes them the most money possible." Roberta retorted with a snort.

"How can they do that?" Tooley would have been more shocked had he not been so tired.

"All I know is that they can and will." she said in a forlorn tone of voice. "I know, hon. It's a real shame. A real shame." Roberta took one last drag off of her cigarette and threw it to the ground. "I better get back or I won't have this job anymore." she said, looking down.

Over in the distance, a couple of cows were laying down for some reason. They may have been suffering from heat exhaustion and thirst because there was a heat advisory in effect for their part of Missouri. Tooley and Roberta focused on them for a second and then a piece of farm equipment drove up to the cows. Someone got out and put a metal snare around their ears. They then got back in and dragged these disabled animals all the way across the rest of the asphalt, about the size of a football field. Tooley and Roberta could hear them screaming in pain the whole way. They were dumped in a pile of dead ones who had perished in the same manner and left to die.

"What in the hell was that?" Tooley exclaimed.

"That's what they do with the sick, injured, and disabled ones. In about two weeks, the cull truck will pick them up." Roberta replied. "They see us helping them and they'll put us out of business!" Roberta cried and ran back to her place.

Tooley ran behind her, spitting on the asphalt. He knew that those cows had been severely scraped across it. He was now more depressed than ever.

CHAPTER TWELVE

"Hello?" Tooley asked after dialing the number for the NYPD.

"Hello, NYPD?" an officer answered in a New York dialect, his voice as pessimistic as a telephone operator's.

"Yes, my mother, May Reynolds, was a victim of a crime a few months ago and I'm her son. I was curious if anybody caught her attacker." Tooley said in a very adult way.

"Ha, ha. What was the victim's name?" he asked as if Tooley was telling a joke.

"May Reynolds." Tooley was starting to feel helpless.

"Let's see here…" the man said out loud. Tooley could hear the clicking of the officer's computer for about a minute. He rolled his eyes in impatience.

"No, son, it doesn't say that the case has been closed. We'll keep searching for him based on a description given by a couple of the witnesses. We'll call you when we track him down." the man laughed at himself. Yet, Tooley felt like he was laughing at him.

"Thanks." Tooley said, most insincerely.

"Have a nice day." the cop mocked just another one of America's citizens and hung up.

"Shoot!" Tooley yelled after he slammed the phone down on the receiver. "I know that he really didn't think they'd find that criminal!" he vented. Tooley then decided that he was not going to even tell his mother that he even tried to find out if the monster was apprehended. May was in the garage fixing something with some tools and was not in the house when Tooley called to get information on the whereabouts of the sick whacko who ruined their getaway.

∗   ∗   ∗

"I'm getting too many conscious ones here, folks!" yelled the sticker, who could barely slit the upcoming cows' throats so he could bleed them. "I'm having to send too many live ones on to the legger and butcher, you pathetic losers!" he was clearly losing patience. Tooley could have heard him bellowing one state away. He felt really bad, but he thought that he most certainly was not a pathetic loser.

"Then someone slow the line down immediately!" Tooley demanded loudly. All of a sudden, the sticker stomped over to the boy and got in his face. "I'll report you for going too slow and costing everyone money." he threatened and went back to slitting maybe only one out of every five cows coming up to his station.

"You are a loser!" Tooley said and ran over to the sticker jerk, and spat in his face. Then he ran outside and paged Jose` on the phone.

"Jose`, could you please slow down the production line down some? The sticker is getting irate with me!" Tooley left in his message.

As Tooley mozied back into his workspace, Jose` was waiting there for him, his arms folded across his chest.

"Tooley, you will no longer be needed at the knock box. Your behavior has become unproductive for our business. You will be working out in the chicken coop collecting dead birds. I'll get Roberta to show you where that is and if you can't get along there, then you will be fired." Jose` let his worker know. Tooley felt a bearlike quality start to want to come out as his face turned to Jose`.

"But the sticker is having trouble doing that many cows! There are animals being skinned and butchered alive, and…" Tooley was rudely cut off.

"That's the way it is. There's nothing you can do to slow down our streamlined production." Jose` flatly informed Tooley. "Roberta, yes, go show Tooley the chicken coop job requirements now." Jose` ordered the lady as she was coming up to the two teenage boys.

"Tooley, hello!" Roberta exclaimed in a way that made Tooley feel recognized for the first time in his so-called career.

"Hi. They want me outta here and for me to work out in the chicken coop." he said, needing just a little sympathy.

"You poor dear." Roberta paused, and took Tooley by the hand. "Come with me. That job just may be more suitable for you anyhow." she led him away from the stern Jose`, carrying Tooley's water jug. As they walked outside to another building, Roberta said "I know why you were having trouble."

"Why?" the boy asked.

"You see how many cows that they want you to send through per minute? They won't stop looking for an employee who will do just that until they find someone. They're constantly replacing people when they've had enough complaints. People who work here are having to witness the law being broken…" Roberta trailed off, feeling like she had said too much.

"What do you mean, Roberta?" Tooley was trying to understand.

"Well, it goes unspoken around here, but, the cows are supposed to be rendered unconscious before slaughter. That was your job. But they expect so many animals to be slaughtered that the Humane Slaughter Act of 1958 is largely ignored." Roberta did not care about what her boss thought of her telling Tooley that.

"The Humane Slaughter Act of 1958?" Tooley repeated in the form of a question.

"Yes! All cows and other animals-which mistakenly excludes chickens-are supposed to be rendered unconscious after they leave the knocker." she explained. "Don't tell anyone that I'm mentioning that law, because if anybody actually enforced the law, the whole production plant here and elsewhere in the United States would be shut down." she went on to tell her new friend.

"So how is it that they can't enforce the law?" Tooley wanted to know in a strong tone.

"Because of all of the deregulation that has been going on since the 1980s. It gives inspectors no power at all, so nothing gets reported hardly ever." she answered him.

"Are you serious?" Tooley asked.

"Dead serious. Pardon the pun." Roberta had seen deregulation all before and what it had done to the people as well as the animals.

"Hummm…" Tooley mumbled. "What it's done to me psychologically could kill me. I don't know if I'll ever enjoy the barbecue down at Minnie's in the same way ever again! That's all I know." Tooley said as they approached a huge, practically windowless building the size of a football field. "And you're saying that if I sued, nothing would be done to change this mental torture?" Tooley was becoming less and less innocent as the passing moments were quickly going by.

"Most likely. Now, you may get a very small amount of money, but nothing would change for the better. Hell, nobody here ever gets the health insurance to cover mental health, much less physical health." Roberta said quietly, feeling bad for Tooley.

"So, how would one try to change things?" Tooley asked her.

"I really couldn't say. Maybe an undercover sting operation?" she sighed. "But that would be so tricky. Even if you brought a camera in the production line, you would receive many threats and the only way they would allow a camera is when they do a tour of it. And that's when they clean up their act, so you most likely wouldn't catch any violations." Roberta unlocked the "chicken coop" "The President of the United States is the only one able to do something, but Beachtown would no longer exist economically without this living hell they call Beachtown Slaughterhouse and Factory Farm." she said in a rather defeated manner. "You could at least e-mail the President a letter explaining why he should do something. "www.thewhitehouse.gov!" she suggested with a smile. She opened the big sliding door. A real warm blast of air smelling of strong ammonia hit Tooley's young snout. It was dark in there.

"Oh, gross!" he cried as he entered the prison of a building. "Roberta, it really stinks in here, woman!"

"That's the scent of waste made by these thousands of trapped birds. Grab a mask." Roberta found one on the polluted ground. "I know it smells horrible, but your job is to look around in all of the cages and remove any dead chickens. This is where the broiler birds are kept." the woman was so tired of showing these underappreciated employees how bad it was in there. She put on a mask and told Tooley that he would need his gloves and trash bags. "The ones on the bottom row lay eggs." Tooley could see a conveyor belt under them, carrying eggs. "And here's a flashlight in case you can't tell the difference between a dead one and a live one." she reported to him. She pointed to where he needed to go. Tooley saw cage upon cage stacked on top of eachother, full of motionless white feathers with red dots in them. An occasional fight amongst them could be heard. "They cut off their beaks so they won't peck eachother to death…Look-those cages are only two feet by two feet. And they cram as many as four or five birds in each. No room even for preening. No room at all." Roberta said and looked at Tooley who was itching for fresh air. "Just open the cage like this and take your finished one and put it in the bag." she closed it back up. "And close it like that."

"Okay, Roberta. When's break?" Tooley asked through the insufficient white cloth mask on his face.

Roberta wanted to laugh but she was busy suffocating. "In a couple of hours, kid." she answered. Tooley collapsed in his soul. He wished to God that he could be enrolling in Washington University. He was eligible for an academic scholarship with all of the excellent grades that he had gotten in high school. "Okay, I've got to go now. But if you have any questions, go to the office and they'll make sure to have them answered." she smiled at Tooley and walked rather quickly out the big door.

"Good." Tooley thought to himself. He could do that just to get fresh air. He looked around not knowing where to start. "Yeah, a letter to the President." he pondered on the idea. He walked over to the first row of cages with some gloves and the flashlight. Roberta was very correct. He had a little trouble seeing each individual chicken.

Holding the bag, he observed no dead bird yet. He noticed that there was a feed dish in each little jail. An angry feeling washed over him as he realized that those birds would have to fight with eachother just to get a chance to have probably a minimal amount of food. He felt a resulting sadness as he knew that some of them ended up starving. "That's where I come in." he told himself. The stench was eating at his lungs as he searched through all of those whitish-brown feathers. He was not sure but he thought that he had spotted a motionless one. He opened the cage where it was and touched it. Another bird squawked at Tooley and tried to escape, but Tooley steadfastly gripped the targeted body to get it in his bag. "It's just trash now." he thought to himself, and closed the cage door on the eager live bird. He hated his job, and searched on for a couple of smelly hours. Almost fainting, Tooley fell to his knees, his palms slapping the ground.

*   *   *

Planning an escape, Tooley set down his trash bag half full of dead hens. Taking off his gloves, he had just ripped the seemingly idiotic mask off of his sweaty face. It was so hot in there that he was about to pass out again amongst the invisible odor. He wiped his forehead with the back of his hand. There was a dark streak of grime near his wrist. He ditched his dead flashlight and ran out of the unforgiving dungeon. It was not time for his break, but he wanted to get out of there. He acted like he had a question and went to the main office, looking for Larry.

Jose` bumped into him in the hallway, and Tooley breathlessly asked for either Larry or Roberta.

"What's the problem?" the underage immigrant from Mexico asked as if Tooley was wasting his time.

"Uh…my flashlight went dead and I need a new one." the former student was impressed with his own quick thinking, for a second.

"Go to Larry's office and he'll know where one is. Happens a lot." Jose` commented and looked away as if he had to go.

"Okay." said Tooley, thinking about his break, his head in the clouds as a result of enjoying fresh air. "See you later." Jose` was already down the hall.

"They hate me." Tooley said softly and then got angry again. "Oh, I'm so lucky that I wasn't fired." he said a little louder, with plenty of sarcasm. Then he went to the office to ask for a replacement flashlight. He took his time in doing that, trying to think about what he was going to do for money instead of this. The boy was determined to keep looking for a job. He thought that it would be cool if the Bingo Hall was hiring.

"That would be a dream!" he exclaimed in a whisper as Larry bumped into him in the doorway.

"Hey, Tooley."Larry acknowleged him firmly, as if the kid had better shape up.

"I need a flashlight, Larry. Either that or some new batteries." he said right away.

"They are in the coop in a drawer. I think it's one of the top ones where the countertop is." Larry directed his worker, and nodded like Tooley was dismissed. He walked away towards where Jose` went, leaving Tooley to head back to the plain building full of fumes. Once again, he took his time and hoped that his mother had found something on her office computer for him.

"After this, I'll ask her when I pick her up, if I'm not too tired to remember." Tooley mumbled, walking slowly. His break was coming right up. It would be only for seven minutes, but it sounded great, like water does when one's thirsty.

The sun continued to melt the day away and five o'clock came around, thankfully. Tooley threw his mask down to the ground where he found it. He burst out the door and closed it. He wondered why it was even kept shut, but he got out of there. He made sure to go to the stodgy office and clock out. On the way, he noticed a pile of trash moving outside of the coop. There was a wounded old chicken thrashing about among the garbage.

"What are you doing here?" Tooley spoke gently to her. He was getting angry again, wondering who would just dump it out in a pile of waste. He grabbed the bird out of it and, not seeing any other ones there, he simply dashed away from the monument of ignorance. He left the factory farm and went for the car. "It's okay." he reassured the chicken and put it in the back seat. It was way too weak to move. "I'll take you out of here. We've got to pick up Mom from work now."

$$* \quad * \quad *$$

"Hey, kid! How've you been doing?" Ginny, Tooley's neighbor, asked after she answered her door. "What you got?"

"Here's Chickee. I want you to have her." Tooley said, handing the old woman the lethargic bird. It had patches of dirt, and oil had soaked its head. The dog could be heard barking out back.

"Well…" Ginny responded kindly, looking a little lost. "Come on in."

"Thanks." Tooley said and, still with Chickie, helped himself to a seat on the couch. "I got a job to help with the bills. It's at the factory farm and slaughterhouse. I found her in a heap of trash by the chicken coop. It's actually a big, disgusting building."

"My dear!" Ginny stopped and looked at the weak thing in Tooley's lap. "I'd be glad to take her. I could try feeding it, but you know, she may not make it much longer. Poor bird." Ginny lamented.

"Yeah. I rescued her. It's like they just threw her away. I just wanted it to be free." Tooley said and handed Chickee over to Ginny.

"She was probably not able to lay eggs anymore and wasn't useful to them. That's what happens over at those places. I've seen a television program about those hens." she pictured and shuddered.

"Probably. I'm not crazy about the job. In fact, I hate it with all of my heart." Tooley tried not to say much more.

"Well…You won't be working there forever. Aren't you up for an academic scholarship, Tooley?" Ginny asked.

"Yes. I was working on that a couple of weeks ago. I want to go to Washington University in St. Louis." Tooley looked away, thinking more about money and work. "I'm lucky that it's my day off. usually I work every day of the week. They're not very understanding of having a day off. I want to quit, but there are no other places to work right now." Tooley explained.

"I know. This town's economy is bad enough, but it seems to be worse right now. I hear Minnie's downtown is going to close at least during the coming winter, and they might not reopen." the neighbor lady gossiped.

"Oh no! Gosh, Ginny… I hope not! I love Minnie's!" Tooley exclaimed and looked down for a minute. "What else are we going to find out?" he was tired of getting riled up every day.

"The whole country feels the pinch right now, I'm afraid." said Ginny with a lilt. "America's supposed to be more fortunate than this. You'd be surprised at the atrocities that are still allowed to happen here and now. A lot has been neglected." Ginny stopped and took a much needed breath of air through her oxygen tank.

"I guess so." Tooley paused and said "Well, I guess I'll be going now. I want to go home and take a long nap. I hope Chickee will have a good rest of her life." Tooley looked at the bird and walked to the front door.

"See you later, child. And try to cheer up!" Ginny ordered, pointing her aged finger at him from the living room.

"Bye." Tooley replied and exited the stuffy little house. He marched over to his and made a trail of melancholy to his bed.

CHAPTER THIRTEEN

"Hey, Tools! Happy Labor Day!" May came into her son's bedroom smiling proudly. He was sleeping in late-as he rightly should be. May felt a warmness inside as she looked at her little boy asnooze under his quilt. The lady sat down on the edge of his bed and ran her fingers through his semi-short dark hair.

"Get out of that! Run!" Tooley was clearly having a nightmare. A nightmare like ones had right before waking if one slept too long.

"Tooley! It's all right! I'm here!" May cried and shook him softly. She did not like to see her son scared. He woke up suddenly and fixed his eyes on May. "You were having a bad dream." she commented.

"Mom! Oh…!" he hollered, his heart beating as fast as a gerbil's heart rate. He sat upright, petrified, and waited until he felt like speaking. "Hi Mom. Oh, thank God it's Labor Day!" exclaimed Tooley.

"Yes. Yes, it is, Tools. I just wanted to thank you for the five hundred dollars you left for me to pay the hospital. I found it on my nightstand. Thank you so very much, baby!" May cried with intense satisfaction. "That's going to help us a lot." she squeezed Tooley's arm. He began to stretch.

"You're very welcome, Mom...Find anything about a different job for me?" asked Tooley with high hopes. May's enthusiasm floated out the door.

"No, son. I still haven't." answered May.

"Oh, okay." Tooley said, about to feel disgusted. "You know, Mom, screw it. I'm going to get 'em." Tooley planned. "He went over his options in his head. The bloodflow of his creativity started to pump more thoroughly as he became more and more conscious.

"Tooley!" May screamed and stood up. She ran to the kitchen and leaned on the counter. She looked out the window. It was so humid that it started to rain, with a clap of shouting thunder. May loved that sound. She loved it so much that she burst out the back door to stand in it. All thoughts including what to do about anything left her for ten glorious minutes. In fact, she cared not if she got washed away. Soaking her blonde hair, the rain made May feel relieved. It made her more relaxed as thunder rolled past the town. She just did not seem to care anymore in those refreshing minutes. Tooley came to the screen and stood there, looking at his mother stretch out her arms. It looked as if she was reaching out to mother nature herself. He let her be and went to the telephone to call Warren.

"Hey, Warren! Guess what?" Tooley said, about to laugh at the sound of Warren's voice.

"What?" his friend asked soberly.

"I wanna get drunk." Tooley was blunt about that.

"Didn't you call me all trashed last night?" Warren reminded Tooley, a little surprised at the statement.

"I don't really care. Wanna get some cold ones?" Tooley pushed on. There was a silence on the end of the line.

"Tooley, I don't know. Who's going to buy it for us, huh?" Warren almost sounded like a cop.

"I don't know. Those were my mom's that I snuck to my room." Tooley said, feeling bad that he would have to beg his mother to buy alcohol. "Yeah. I don't know. It just sounds so good. It gives me some relief.!" he confessed.

"Yeah. Maybe some other time." Warren said and added "So, Tooley, how have you been doing?" he was a little worried. "What's up?"

"Me at seven o'clock every morning." Tooley giggled. "No…Well, yeah, I'm still working, trying to help out my mom. The college may have to wait. I may not get the scholarship, but if it can wait a semester…" he lost what he might have said.

"Oh. How's work going?" Warren quizzed on.

"It sure is work. It's really hard work. My mom is trying to find something else for me everyday, but nothing seems to come up for me. Not even a job at a barnyard or something." Tooley rolled his eyes.

"Gosh. That's not good." Warren felt bad for his best friend, but did not know what else to say.

"That's probably why I just want to get plastered." Tooley explained in sort of a cynical way. To Warren, he sounded a little older than the kid he went to school with.

"Well, you just call me whenever you need a drink. Anytime, even if it's late or early. Okay? I'm your best friend, Tooley." Warren demanded.

"Okay." Tooley said, appreciating that Warren cared.

"And I hope you find something else really soon." he said nicely.

"Me too. So, what are you doing?" Tooley asked.

"Oh, nothing, I guess." he sighed. "Amy wanted me to take her to the library for a movie. A bunch of her friends wanted to meet her there. You know, they have movies for kids sometimes and so I took her." Warren said kind of drudgingly.

"Oh. That sounds very nice!" Tooley replied, a little jealous that he had no brothers or sisters.

"Yeah. Some movie for girls." Warren said, and laughed.

"Hey, War." Tooley was just now getting to his plan. He was a little scared, but he asked anyhow.

"Yes?" Warren answered, not knowing what he was going to ask him.

"Will you let me borrow you digital cam-corder?" asked Tooley, not sounding scared.

"Ummm, yeah; what are you going to do with it?" wondered Warren, whinnying. He could only imagine.

"I need it. I'm going to try and do my own documentary." Tooley stated, as serious as a tiger going for a zookeeper's pants.

"Okay…What kind of documentary?!" Warren was suddenly excited.

"Just something that I'd like to record. Can I please just use it?" Tooley felt that he could explain later what exactly he was going to do.

"Yeah. Come over." Warren affirmed.

"See you in ten minutes." Tooley planned.

By the time Tooley got off of the telephone with his friend, May approached the boy, dripping wet and feeling calmer.

"Hi, Mom. I'm going over to Warren's to visit him. I'll be back within an hour, okay?" Tooley told and asked.

"All right, son. Have a good time." May agreed. She wanted Tooley to stay in touch with his friends." Be careful, sweetie. Bye!" his mother exclaimed, watching her son go out to the garage. The rain was letting up as Tooley backed out of the mushy driveway. He drove out towards the neighborhoods near the main street of Beachtown. He turned down Clydesdale Drive and pulled into a driveway whose house looked like a seventies style split level structure.

Tooley practically made a rampage to the oak and glass paneled front door, stepping on a row of impatiens that Warren's mother had planted in April with loving gloved hands. He felt bad, but his idea had taken over any feelings of guilt from some flowers. Excitement had taken hold of Tooley's brain and he thought that he could make up for the flowers later. He struck the doorbell. It made a chime sound and within moments, Warren stumbled to the doorknob. He turned it quickly and let his guest in the dwelling. Warren had the object of Tooley's desire hanging over his shoulder.

"Hi, Tools." Warren greeted him.

"Hi. I appreciate this very much. I'll bring it back in maybe a week or two. Thanks." Tooley had accepted the camera from Warren and put it over his shoulder. "I'll have it back in one piece!" Tooley promised and turned to go.

"Hey! What are you going to film?" Warren yelled.

"That's something that I'll have to tell you about later. After I'm finished." Tooley commanded and walked back to the Saturn. He could not wait to start on the exposure of his working conditions.

"Okay!" Warren exclaimed and shut the door, shaking his head in anticipation of what he would be told later.

Driving with the camera in the passenger's seat, Tooley blasted the radio, enjoying his day off and felt glad that Warren was being so supportive. "He won't be sorry." Tooley thought in his adolescent mind. Now he was all ready to report to his job the next day.

✳   ✳   ✳

Tooley was awake about twenty minutes before the alarm clock startled him. He depressed the off button and sat up, taking in the sight of the black leather case sitting in the corner of the bedroom. He took a deep breath and thought it was a break to not have to take his mother to work, since it was her one day off for at least ten days.

Tooley reached for the knob on his top dresser drawer and went on to get ready for work. May was not up yet, so he made a sack lunch and grabbed a gallon jug of his usual daily water. Remembering the camera, the boy ran down the little hallway to get it out of his room. The car keys were in plain sight on the floor. He grabbed them and left the house with a smirk. Getting into the car, Tooley started to become nervous about how he was going to introduce his problems on camera. He got the instrument out of its luggage and turned the power on. hitting the record button, Tooley aimed the lens at himself, at a safe distance- "My name is Tooley Reynolds, and I just graduated from high school. I'm seventeen years old and work at the Beachtown Slaughterhouse and Factory Farm. I'm on my way to a job that pays no health insurance to their employees. They get about one day off every month. Let's take a look." he reported and shut off the recorder.

Tooley felt okay so he drove away, heading towards the unwanted place of employment. He wished that he had Warren helping him with all of the unfamiliar buttons. It would also have helped to have someone film while he was talking. Tooley came to the conclusion that it would not really matter.

"Just as long as I can explain what is being recorded as I record it." said Tooley out loud, trying to decide how he would start.

Almost in the parking lot, Tooley started to look around to see if anybody noticed his presence. He did not feel any immediate danger and went on to pull into the parking lot of the subject of his documentary.

He knew that he wanted to film the entryway to the slaughterhouse, since the name of the whole operation was on that part of the compound. Exiting the car, the boy snatched up the recording device from the front passenger seat. Tooley had his eyes peeled for anybody who might be suspicious.. He just kept the camera bag on his shoulder and waited for anybody to leave the front doors.

After about a minute, nobody was seen, so Tooley scooped the camera out of the case and aimed its lens at the front entryway, recording the sign that stated the name of the place. It said: Beachtown Slaughterhouse and Factory Farm.

Tooley quickly filmed only that and pushed the stop button. The next thing he needed to do was clock in at the chicken cages, somehow hiding the protruding graduation gift of Warren's. He needed to be careful not to break it. He was afraid that somebody would find him filming and bust it into a hundred worthless pieces. "Well…" Tooley thought, "I just have to want to try to do this." So he walked casually out to where he was due to clock into his job. Usually, only one other person is in the coop, and that is the feeder. Tooley figured that he had a couple of hours to get some footage of how awful conditions at the factory farm were. At least he could show that with little risk of being caught.

Tooley opened the doors where the hens were still being ignored. The smell of roses was absent in there. What was present was the odor of ammonia. Tooley lifted the camera out of its bag once again and held his flashlight in one hand. He turned back the flashlight and the digital camera on and shone the light on some nearby chickens, their claws wounded from the wire bottomed cages.

"This is the factory farm where I work full time. The chickens here spend their whole lives here in cages too cramped for them to even move or ever eat a reasonable amount of food in. My job is to remove dead birds from all of these stacked cages. You can see here how their feet and bottoms have horrible, infected pressure sores." Tooley got a shot of the tremendous amount of chickens living this way.

"The smell of ammonia is so thick that I have nearly passed out from it working here with only two seven minute breaks every day. I hardly have time to eat my lunch. I'm starting to develop a cough that I know had been caused by the filth and chemicals in the air." He slowly walked by each row of cages until he reached the other side of the ominous coop.

"Some of these chickens will be slaughtered, and some will provide eggs. I will show you what happens when a hen is too old and useless to produce enough eggs. She ends up over here." Tooley pointed to a huge landfill behind the factory farm. He paced over to it, tripping over a couple of rocks, making the camera slip a little. He filmed part of the landfill where some barely live birds were flailing around amongst dead ones, all stuffed in with viscera and other waste. "She will be left for dead and to suffer a slow and diseased death. The smell right here is too disgusting for words." Tooley backed himself and the lens away from the sorry excuse for a final resting place. He turned off the new camera and looked around, as paranoid as a polar bear in the tropics.

He took himself back to the so-called chicken farm and set to work, putting the camera and its sachel in a good hiding place. Glad that nobody witnessed the first part of the documentary, Tooley wiped his brow to get the sweat of nervousness off of his face. It was to be rather hot that day, even if it was now after Labor Day. Tooley could not wait for his break in a few hours. He schemed and made mental arrangements to try to figure out how he was ever going to clear the slaughterhouse. Knowing that everyone took their seven minute break at the same time, he thought that he could record the cows right before everybody quit for their short breaks. He thought that maybe it would give him a chance to get out of the slaughterhouse right when everybody was busy leaving their stations. He was not positive that he would get away without a fight, but he felt more sure that his plan would have a good chance to work somewhat according to how he was forseeing his move.

✳   ✳   ✳

Tooley was in the midst of his dead chicken removal job just as the person who fed the birds came in to give a very minimal amount of feed to them. Tooley saw the portions of what four birds were expected to share, clamped inside their cages; they were fed with feeders and small water bottles that looked like they were for mice.

He waited until the feeder was gone, and began to wait for the break. He kept on doing his work, about ready to pass out once again because of the lack of fresh air. He dropped his bag and ran to the jug of water he had filled before his long shift. He grabbed it up, opened it as fast as he could, and quenched his unforgiving thirst, swallowing the water over and over again, it dripping down his face and neck. Tooley was content in the hydration. He let out a refreshed sigh, and put the jug down. The digital clock on his watch said that it was about a few minutes until break time. His hands felt a prickle of perspiration and there were fireflies in his stomach.

Quickly, he took the camera out of its hiding place and walked really fast out of the building toward the slaughterhouse, where everyone was about to go on their miniature breaks. He made it all the way to the doors, filming as he got closer. He stopped while still recording and dared said "Here is a slaughterhouse where the Humane Slaughter Act of 1958 is not enforced, on a daily basis. Let's look closer at where this actually happens." Tooley stopped the camera, using haste to get it back into its bag. Now all that he had to do was wait for everybody to go on their break and get out of there. He felt vulnerable standing there with equipment hanging on his shoulder.

Roberta came out of the doors first and noticed the kid.

"Hey, want a cigarette, Tooley?" she did not seem to act like anything seemed abnormal.

"Sure, Roberta. Thanks!" Tooley thought it was lucky that she asked that. Now he could go to his car to "smoke" it. That would give him something to do. She handed him one and smiled.

"Your welcome! I gotta go out to the bathroom! See you!" said Roberta, her desire to go written all over her face.

"See you!" Tooley said as he put the cigarette in his mouth and walked toward his car. He wanted to watch from there to make sure most everyone was going out of the door. Once he got there, he spied where workers were now leaving the building for their breaks.

"Okay, come on, come on...Get outta there!" Tooley whispered to himself, getting ready to walk right back to the doors, which were opening less and less. He unzipped the camera baggage and put his trembling hand on the object inside so that he could rapidly get it out at any time. Keeping the cancer stick gripped in his lips, he walked as fast as he could without running back to the slaughterhouse. If it was freezing cold outside, Tooley's hands would be just as sweaty as they were now. He was scared.

CHAPTER FOURTEEN

As Tooley had less and less time to waste, he opened the door and walked right on in. He saw nobody in the hall so far, but he knew that at any second the wrong person could approach. He dashed through those two sets of heavy double iron doors and, getting out the camera, recorded the whole production place where the cows met their fate. He scanned the plant from one side to the other, not being suspicious to anybody. The sound of metal clanking against metal could be picked up on the film. "The cattle are taken here to be slaughtered in the production line by hardworking employees." Tooley wanted to familiarize an audience with the factory. Then he heard somebody who sounded like Larry open the doors. Tooley ran to the wall where one of the iron doors opened up against it. He stopped the recording and stood there, his back pressed firmly to the wall. His heart pounded in his chest, thumping hard in his ears. Tooley licked his lips, hoping that Larry would not see him. He tried to look for another hiding place. He spotted piles of boxes stacked on pallets. He sped over and crouched between them, waiting to see what Larry was doing. He saw him go into another door on the other side of the work areas.

 Iaminterdifferenti

Tooley had no time now. He prayed to himself that he did and got himself over to the cow disassembly line.

"Here is where the knocker is supposed to zap the cows unconscious, between the eyes, with a bolt gun. The voltage is always set too low by the bosses and the bolt gun only gets the job done way less than half of the time. The speed of the line is so fast that the knocker has no choice but to let live cattle accidentally go on through consciously to the sticker, who has to hang them up and slit their throats. Problem is, they even go through without having their throats slit and go on to be skinned and gutted alive! This happens a lot of the time, the cows don't' get unconscious properly and at that line speed, they go through unnecessary torture being literally taken apart piece by piece all very much alive." Tooley pointed the camera at each station as he explained the problem. "Maybe one day the Humane Slaughter Act of 1958 will be taken more seriously for the mercy of not only the cattle, but for the employees who must see this day in and day out. The production line must be slowed down and the voltage on the knocking gun must be turned up." Tooley stopped filming and put the cam-corder away over his shoulder. "Surely nobody could hear me!" he whispered as he looked around.

All of two seconds went by and Tooley walked to the door where everyone escaped to go on breaks or to go home. He tried turning the knob, but it was locked "Darn!" Tooley was having more angst building up in his throat. "I guess break isn't quite over." he thought to himself. Then he heard Jose`'s voice yell, "Hey! You're not supposed to be in here! It's breaktime!"

Tooley turned around and sprinted towards the iron doors that he came in from. Jose` was hot on his tracks, catching up quite quickly to Tooley. Tooley opened one of the iron doors and attempted to run past the doorway when the bag got stuck on one of the levers. Jose` grabbed at it while Tooley tried getting the camera bag loose. "Let go!" Tooley demanded, wanting to get out of that building, holding onto the leather strap. Jose` had ahold of the part containing the camera, loosening it from the doorhandle. Tug of war was the game that they started to play.

Since Jose` had ahold of the part of the bag containing the camera, he held firmly onto it with overly developed biceps. He looked for where the bag would open. At that second, Tooley pulled even harder, adrenaline flowing through his ever tense body. Tooley got the whole bag loose from Jose`'s disapproving grip at that point of Jose`'s somewhat divided attention. Then Tooley opened the door that they just came through and ran back onto the slaughter floor, moving his legs as fast as he ever did in years. The workers were back from their break and were so busily working that they did not even notice the boy running towards them. Jose` was on the chase, wanting that camera.

"Hey! You had no permission to film here!" he yelled as he came through the doors. Tooley was almost to the exit door that had been locked earlier during the break. The next thing that the striving journalist knew, he was on the bloody floor next to the sticker. He had slipped and fell. His head hit it hard, and Jose` was catching up fast. Tooley, still conscious, turned his head to see that he was, indeed, on the floor. He knew that he had to get up fast, and did so, the side of his face the color of crimson. His clothes were partially soaked in cow blood. Rapidly pacing toward the exit door, he fell again, his shoes slippery from the fluid. He held onto the camera case desperately, and jumped up, Jose` coming into his peripheral vision.

"Larry, call the police right now! We have some trouble." Jose` said on a cell phone as Tooley opened the door. "Tooley, give me the camera!" he shouted and started speaking Spanish.

Tooley stumbled out of the establishment, going in the direction of the parking lot. He tried to run fast and go hide amongst the cars, getting away with the camera.

Larry had come down to the floor to see where Jose` was.

"Jose`! What's going on?" he asked hurriedly.

"It's Tooley…! He's been filming the place!" said Jose` in an excited series of words. "He went out the exit door!"

Larry was startled at the idea, afraid of what Tooley had filmed. He headed out the door and looked for him. "Shoot!" Larry exclaimed.

Meanwhile, Tooley had found a hiding place between a blue Ford Taurus and an older red Pontiac Grand Am. He was feeling very weak and had no idea when someone would find him. He crouched down and waited.

"Don't just stand there, Jose`, go find him!" Larry screamed desperately, like a little boy having a fit in a department store when his mother told him that he could not have a certain toy. At that second, the police arrived in the parking lot, their lights appropriate for hosting a party at a skating rink. Jose` was running toward the columns of cars, trying to see where Tooley had gone with the tape and camera.

The policemen swiftly got out of their car and aimed their pistols at Jose`.

"Pow!….Pow!" said both of their guns.

"No!" Larry yelled, as if his voice could stop what he was afraid was going to happen.

Down Jose` went, after bullets made bloody Swiss cheese of his torso and upper body. "No!" yelled Larry a second time. The cops stood there, believing that they had caught the criminal who had no permit to film the slaughterhouse.

The illegal Mexican immigrant who was under the age of eighteen lay in the parking lot. Tooley made a run for it into the woods unscathed as the police went to look at Jose`'s body. It was on the ground next to a car with bullet holes in its windshield.

"You morons! That's not the guy!" Larry started to fight verbally. "That's not the cameraman!"

The two policemen strutted towards Larry. "It's not?" said one of them.

"No. You shot Jose' He was just a kid." Larry finally broke down in tears. "My best worker."

"A kid? You hired somebody who was underage?" asked one officer.

"No…I…he was a volunteer." Larry lied sheepishly. He knew that he was now in trouble.

The other officer said "He looked Hispanic. Then he asked "He legal?"

Larry remained silent as a mute during a snowstorm.

"Okay. Get him downtown." said the same officer to the other. "We need to file a summons. And call an ambulance for the boy."

"You going to cut me another deal?" asked Larry as they were walking towards the car. The officers looked at each other and laughed.

THE END

The Humane Slaughter Act of 1958

The federal law requiring that all swine, sheep, cattle, and horses be humanely handled and rendered unconscious prior to being shackled, hoisted, and bled at slaughterhouses

CPSIA information can be obtained at www.ICGtesting.com
Printed in the USA
BVOW070947190412

288032BV00001B/22/P